The Snowflake Chronicle Christmas Adventures

Freya Jobe

Published by Freya Jobe, 2024.

This is a work of fiction. Similarities to real people, places, or events are entirely coincidental.

THE SNOWFLAKE CHRONICLE CHRISTMAS ADVENTURES

First edition. November 19, 2024.

ISBN: 979-8230425243

Written by Freya Jobe.

The Snowflake Chronicles
37 Christmas Adventures

Every snowflake carries a story. Whispering as it falls, it brings with it a sprinkle of magic, a touch of wonder, and the promise of adventure. In The Snowflake Chronicles: 37 Christmas Adventures, each tale unfolds like a delicate flurry, spinning stories of courage, kindness, laughter, and love—all wrapped in the spirit of Christmas.

This collection of short stories is your passport to a world of holiday enchantment. From the bustling workshops of the North Pole to snowy forests where animals prepare for their winter feast, and from twinkling city streets to the quiet serenity of nativity scenes, each adventure celebrates the joy and magic of the Christmas season. You'll meet mischievous elves, talking snowmen, brave little reindeer, and even a few surprising visitors from far-off lands.

These stories are perfect for cozy nights by the fire, bedtime readings, or festive family gatherings. Each one invites children (and the young at heart) to pause, dream, and rediscover the true meaning of Christmas—whether it's found in a selfless act of kindness, the sparkle of the first snowfall, or the laughter of friends and family.

Chapter 1: A Christmas Catastrophe

Snowflakes danced in the frigid air as a golden glow spilled from the windows of Santa's workshop. Inside, the air was filled with laughter, clanging tools, and the hum of Christmas carols. The elves were hard at work, putting the final touches on toys, stuffing stockings, and wrapping gifts in bright paper adorned with candy canes and snowmen.

Pepper, one of the youngest elves at the North Pole, zipped from one end of the workshop to the other, delivering spools of ribbon and double-checking Santa's famous Naughty and Nice List. Her red hat was slightly too big for her, and it flopped over her eyes as she ran. She pushed it up with a sigh.

"Careful, Pepper!" an older elf named Tinsel called as she walked by, balancing a stack of wooden trains. "You don't want to trip over those little legs of yours!"

Pepper laughed. "If I had longer legs, I'd be twice as fast!" She darted past Tinsel, narrowly avoiding a tower of teddy bears.

All around her, the workshop buzzed with excitement. It was Christmas Eve, the most important night of the year. Santa's sleigh was being prepped outside, his reindeer were eating their final meal of magical oats, and soon the jolly old man himself would be on his way to deliver presents to children around the world.

But as Pepper rushed to the back of the workshop to fetch a fresh roll of wrapping paper, she overheard a conversation that stopped her in her tracks.

"Santa's bag is gone," someone whispered in a low, worried voice.

Pepper's ears perked up. She crept closer, hiding behind a stack of rocking horses to eavesdrop.

"It's not just gone," said a second voice, trembling. "It's missing. Completely vanished."

Pepper's heart skipped a beat. Santa's bag—his magical, bottomless sack that carried gifts for every child—was the single most important thing on Christmas Eve. Without it, there would be no Christmas.

"Do we tell Santa?" the first voice asked.

"Not yet," said the second. "We'll keep looking. It must be around here somewhere."

Pepper ducked out of sight as the two elves walked past, their faces pale with worry. Her mind raced. How could Santa's bag disappear? It was always kept in his sleigh, ready for the big night.

Her hands clenched into fists. She couldn't just stand by and let Christmas fall apart. If the other elves couldn't find the bag, she would. Pepper, the smallest and fastest elf in the workshop, would make sure Christmas went on as planned.

Pepper slipped out of the workshop, pulling her scarf tight against the biting wind. Outside, the sleigh gleamed under the soft light of the northern sky. The reindeer were harnessed and ready, their bells jingling softly as they stamped their hooves. But the large platform where Santa's bag should have been was empty.

"Blitzen!" Pepper called, running up to the nearest reindeer. "Have you seen Santa's bag?"

Blitzen shook his head. "Not since yesterday, when Santa packed it up. It was right there on the sleigh."

Pepper frowned. "Did anyone come near it?"

"Only Santa and Bernard," Blitzen said, referring to the head elf who oversaw the workshop. "But Bernard went back inside hours ago."

Pepper nodded, her mind working furiously. If the bag had been packed yesterday, it must have disappeared sometime between then and now. That meant someone—or something—had taken it.

"Thank you, Blitzen," she said, patting the reindeer's nose. "I'll figure this out."

Back inside the workshop, Pepper searched for Bernard. She found him near the toy trains, directing a group of elves as they loaded them into crates.

"Bernard!" she called, running up to him. "I need to ask you something."

Bernard looked down at her, his thick eyebrows furrowing. "What is it, Pepper? Can't you see I'm busy?"

"It's about Santa's bag," Pepper said in a hushed voice. "Blitzen said you were the last person to see it."

Bernard's expression shifted, his eyes darting around the room. "What are you talking about?" he said quickly. "The bag is on the sleigh, where it always is."

"No, it's not," Pepper said firmly. "It's missing."

Bernard's face turned pale. "Missing? That's impossible!"

"It's true," Pepper said. "I overheard some elves talking about it. If we don't find it soon, Christmas will be ruined."

Bernard rubbed his chin, his expression grim. "This is bad. Very bad. If the bag isn't in the workshop or on the sleigh, it could be anywhere."

"Then we have to start looking now," Pepper said. "Every second counts."

Bernard hesitated for a moment, then nodded. "You're right. We'll split up. You check outside the workshop, and I'll search Santa's office. If you find anything, let me know immediately."

Pepper nodded and darted away, her heart pounding. She didn't have a plan yet, but she knew she couldn't give up. Somewhere out there, Santa's bag was waiting to be found.

Pepper began her search in the snowy courtyard outside the workshop. The area was crisscrossed with footprints from busy elves and reindeer, but nothing seemed out of place. She checked behind snowbanks, under sleighs, and even in the storage shed where spare harnesses were kept. But there was no sign of the bag.

As she was about to give up, she spotted something unusual near the edge of the courtyard: a trail of glittering red fabric, partially buried in the snow. Her heart leapt. Could it be?

She ran over and pulled the fabric free. It wasn't the bag—but it was a scrap of cloth that looked like it had been torn from it. The edges were jagged, and there was a faint trace of golden thread running through it, just like the embroidery on Santa's bag.

Pepper's eyes narrowed. Someone—or something—had dragged the bag out of the courtyard. But who? And why?

She looked around, searching for more clues. A set of faint footprints led away from the fabric, heading toward the dark forest beyond the workshop. The tracks were too small to belong to Santa or any of the reindeer, and they didn't look like elf footprints either. They were strange—long and narrow, with claw-like marks at the tips.

Pepper's stomach twisted with unease. Whatever had taken the bag wasn't from the North Pole.

For a moment, Pepper considered going back to tell Bernard what she had found. But she hesitated. The other elves were busy preparing for Christmas, and they needed to stay focused. If she ran back now, precious time would be wasted.

No, she thought. I'll follow the trail myself. I'm small, I'm fast, and I won't let anything stop me.

With that, Pepper tightened her scarf, squared her shoulders, and stepped into the forest. The trees loomed tall and shadowy around her, their branches heavy with snow. The trail of footprints wound deeper into the woods, leading her toward an adventure she could never have imagined.

As she followed the trail, Pepper couldn't shake the feeling that someone—or something—was watching her. The air grew colder, the shadows darker, and the wind whispered through the trees like a distant voice.

But Pepper didn't turn back. She was determined to find Santa's bag, no matter what. Christmas depended on it.

Little did she know, her bravery would soon be tested in ways she had never dreamed—and the fate of Christmas would rest entirely in her tiny hands.

Chapter 2: The Forest's Wish

Deep in the heart of Silverwood Forest, where snow blanketed the ground like a soft, shimmering quilt, a group of woodland animals gathered in a small clearing. The forest was alive with the scents of pine and winterberries, and the air hummed with excitement. For weeks, the animals had been preparing for a very special celebration: their annual Christmas gathering.

The animals had built a magnificent tree in the center of the clearing, decorated with pinecones dusted in gold, strings of cranberries and popcorn, and glittering icicles made from frozen dew. The squirrels had tied little bows from bits of fabric, the birds had woven nests of twigs and holly, and even the foxes had helped by gathering shiny stones to scatter around the tree's base.

But as beautiful as the tree was, something was missing.

"We need a star," said Bella, the little brown rabbit with a twitching nose. She stood on her hind legs, gazing up at the top of the towering tree. "Every Christmas tree needs a star to shine at the very top!"

The animals murmured in agreement. A tree without a star was like a sky without the moon—lovely, but not quite complete.

"Where are we going to find a star?" asked Oliver, a plump raccoon with a striped tail. "It's not like we can pluck one out of the sky."

"I heard the humans in the village have stars for their trees," said Wren, a tiny bird with feathers as grey as the winter clouds. "They make them out of shiny metal or sparkling glass."

"But we're in the forest," said Luna, the wise old owl perched on a branch above them. "We don't have metal or glass. We'll have to find something that feels like our star—something special and unique."

The animals looked at one another, their faces lighting up with determination. They would find the perfect star for their tree, no matter what it took.

The next morning, the animals divided into groups to begin their search. Bella the rabbit hopped alongside her friend Jasper the fox, while Oliver the raccoon and Wren the bird teamed up to search the treetops. Luna the owl stayed behind to keep watch over the tree and direct the search.

Bella and Jasper began their hunt near the frozen river. The sunlight sparkled on the icy surface, and Bella's ears perked up with excitement. "Look, Jasper! The ice shines just like a star!"

Jasper padded closer and examined the ice. "It's beautiful," he admitted, "but it's too cold and fragile. It would melt or break before we could even get it on the tree."

Bella sighed, her breath puffing in the chilly air. "You're right. Let's keep looking."

Meanwhile, Oliver and Wren scoured the tallest trees in the forest. Wren flew high above the branches, her sharp eyes scanning for anything that sparkled or shone.

"Over here!" she chirped, spotting a patch of snow that glimmered in the sunlight. But when Oliver climbed up to investigate, he shook his head.

"It's just snow," he said. "Pretty, but it won't last."

As the day wore on, the animals grew more and more discouraged. They found many beautiful things—a crystal-clear icicle, a cluster of frost-covered holly berries, even a patch of golden moss—but nothing seemed quite right for their star.

That evening, the animals returned to the clearing, tired and empty-handed. The tree stood tall and beautiful, but its bare top seemed to reach for the stars in vain.

"We looked everywhere," said Bella, her ears drooping. "There's nothing in the forest that can be our star."

Luna the owl hooted softly, her golden eyes glowing in the darkness. "Sometimes, when you can't find what you're looking for, it means you need to create it yourself."

"But how can we create a star?" asked Oliver. "We don't have anything shiny or sparkly."

Luna spread her wings and gestured to the clearing around them. "Look around. The forest is full of gifts. If we work together, we can make something truly special."

The animals exchanged hopeful glances. Luna was right. They didn't need to find a star—they could make one.

The next morning, the clearing buzzed with activity as the animals set to work. Bella and Jasper gathered twigs and branches, carefully tying them together with vines to form the shape of a star. Wren flew high and low, collecting the brightest red berries and golden leaves she could find to decorate it. Oliver scoured the forest floor for shards of quartz and pieces of shiny mica, which he polished with snow until they gleamed.

Even the other animals pitched in. The deer lent their antlers to reach high branches, the squirrels collected strands of spider silk to make the star shimmer, and the beavers chewed the twigs into neat, precise edges.

Finally, after hours of work, the star was complete. It wasn't made of gold or glass, but it was dazzling in its own way. The twigs formed a perfect star shape, the berries and leaves added bursts of color, and the polished stones sparkled like tiny fragments of light.

"It's beautiful," Bella whispered, her eyes wide with awe.

"Let's put it on the tree!" said Oliver, his striped tail twitching with excitement.

With Luna's guidance, the animals worked together to lift the star to the very top of the tree. The moment it was in place, a soft glow seemed to surround it, as if the forest itself was smiling.

That night, the animals gathered in the clearing to admire their work. The tree was radiant, its decorations glistening in the moonlight, and the handmade star at the top shone with a quiet, natural beauty.

"It's perfect," said Bella, snuggling close to Jasper. "It's the perfect star for our tree."

"It's more than perfect," said Luna, her voice soft. "It's a symbol of what makes Christmas special—working together, sharing what we have, and finding beauty in the simple things."

The animals nodded, their hearts full of warmth and joy. As they sang carols and shared winterberries under the starlit sky, they knew that this Christmas would be one they'd never forget.

And above them, the forest's star glowed, a testament to the magic of friendship, teamwork, and the true spirit of the season.

The End.

The Smallest Reindeer

Chapter 3: Too Small to Matter

The snow fell gently over the North Pole, blanketing everything in a sparkling white sheet. Inside Santa's Reindeer Barn, the team of famous flyers—Dasher, Dancer, Prancer, and the rest—were busy preparing for Christmas Eve. The barn was bustling with excitement, but in a tiny stall at the very end, a small reindeer named Pip watched the commotion with a heavy heart.

Pip was the smallest reindeer in the North Pole. He was smaller than the youngest of the trainee reindeer and barely came up to Dasher's shoulder. His antlers were still stubby, and his hooves clicked softly on the icy floor when he walked. Every year, he hoped he'd get a chance to join the sleigh team, and every year, he was told the same thing.

"You're just too small, Pip," Santa's stable master, Gus, had said that morning. "Flying in the sleigh team is a big job. You need strength, speed, and stamina to pull that heavy sleigh through the sky. Maybe next year."

Next year. It was always next year. Pip had heard it so many times, he didn't even feel disappointed anymore—just tired of being overlooked. He wasn't even invited to the final practice run that afternoon.

As the other reindeer trotted off to the training field, Pip stayed behind, alone in the barn. He shuffled over to the hay pile and flopped down with a sigh.

Pip was busy feeling sorry for himself when a cheerful voice called out, "Why the long face, little guy?"

Startled, Pip sat up and turned toward the door. A small, sprightly elf was standing there, her green hat slightly askew and her cheeks pink from the cold. She carried a toolbox over one shoulder and a peppermint stick in the other hand.

"Who are you?" Pip asked.

"Name's Jingle," the elf said with a grin. "I'm the sleigh mechanic. I keep Santa's ride in tip-top shape. And you must be Pip, the little reindeer everyone talks about."

Pip blinked in surprise. "They talk about me?"

"Of course!" Jingle said, plopping down next to him. "I've heard all about your speed and agility. Gus says you can outmanoeuvre any reindeer in the barn."

Pip's ears perked up. "He said that?"

"Sure did," Jingle said. "So why are you sitting here looking glum instead of out there showing the team what you can do?"

Pip's ears drooped again. "Because I'm too small. They don't think I'm strong enough to pull the sleigh."

Jingle tilted her head thoughtfully. "Maybe. But being small has its advantages, you know. Sometimes, what seems like a weakness can turn out to be your greatest strength."

Before Pip could ask what she meant, the barn doors burst open, and Gus came rushing in, his face pale.

"Emergency!" he shouted. "The sleigh team's practice route is blocked by a snowstorm, and the new navigation system is broken. We need to get it fixed before Santa's flight tonight!"

Jingle jumped to her feet. "That's my cue! Where's the sleigh?"

"It's stuck in Snowdrift Valley," Gus said, wringing his hands. "But the snowstorm is too thick for the big reindeer to get through. We don't know how to reach it."

"I can do it!" Pip said suddenly, standing up.

Gus and Jingle turned to look at him.

"I'm small enough to fit through tight spaces, and I'm fast," Pip said, his voice firm. "Let me try."

Gus hesitated, but Jingle grinned. "He's right. If anyone can make it through, it's Pip."

Gus sighed and nodded. "All right, Pip. The sleigh team is counting on you."

Minutes later, Pip stood at the edge of Snowdrift Valley, the wind howling around him. Snow whipped through the air in fierce gusts, but he didn't let it scare him. With a deep breath, he spread his small wings and leapt into the storm.

The icy wind tugged at his fur, but Pip pushed forward, his hooves kicking through the snow. The storm was so thick, he could barely see, but his sharp eyes caught glimpses of the trail ahead—twisting between snow-covered rocks and narrow ice passages.

"This is why I'm here," Pip told himself, dodging a low-hanging branch. "I can fit where the big reindeer can't."

As he climbed higher into the valley, he spotted the sleigh. It was half-buried in snow, its runners stuck in the ice. The big red bag of presents sat in the back, and the navigation system blinked faintly from the dashboard.

"I found it!" Pip shouted, his voice barely audible over the wind.

Pip hurried to the sleigh and began digging out the snow with his hooves. It was slow work, but he didn't stop. His small size made it easier to manoeuvre around the sleigh, and before long, the runners were free.

Now came the hard part. Jingle had given him instructions for resetting the navigation system, but Pip had to climb onto the sleigh to reach it. He scrambled up, his hooves slipping on the icy surface.

"Come on, Pip," he muttered to himself. "You can do this."

Finally, he reached the dashboard. Following Jingle's instructions, he flipped a series of switches and pressed a glowing button. The navigation system beeped and lit up, its map flickering to life.

"Yes!" Pip cheered. "It's working!"

But his celebration was short-lived. A loud cracking noise echoed through the valley, and Pip realized the ice beneath the sleigh was breaking. He had to move fast.

He leapt off the sleigh, spread his wings, and flew ahead of it, guiding it back down the trail. The sleigh slid after him, its runners gliding smoothly over the snow. Pip darted through narrow gaps and under low branches, leading the sleigh out of the storm and back to safety.

When Pip returned to the barn with the sleigh, the other reindeer erupted into cheers. Gus ran up to him, his eyes wide with amazement.

"You did it, Pip!" he said. "You saved the sleigh!"

Jingle grinned as she inspected the sleigh. "And the navigation system is good as new. Great work, Pip."

Santa himself arrived moments later, his red coat dusted with snow. He knelt down in front of Pip and smiled.

"I heard what you did, little one," Santa said, his eyes twinkling. "You proved today that being small doesn't mean being unimportant. In fact, it's often the smallest among us who make the biggest difference."

Pip's heart swelled with pride. For the first time, he didn't feel small—he felt strong, brave, and important.

That night, as Santa prepared for his Christmas flight, Pip was given a special honour. He was named an official member of the sleigh team and took his place at the front, leading the way with his speed and agility.

As they soared into the starry sky, Pip looked down at the North Pole, glowing softly below. He had proven that even the smallest reindeer could do great things—and he knew this was a Christmas he'd never forget.

The End

Chapter 4: The Naughty Elf

Tumble was not your ordinary elf. While the other elves at Santa's Workshop were busy making toys, painting trains, or stuffing stockings, Tumble was always up to something mischievous. His pranks were legendary around the North Pole. One time, he replaced all the candy canes in the workshop with sticks of red-and-white striped celery. Another time, he tied all of Santa's boots together, causing quite a commotion when the big man tried to take his morning stroll.

"Tumble, why don't you ever help?" his friend Glitter asked one day as she polished a shiny red fire truck. "Christmas is about giving, not goofing off."

"I am helping," Tumble replied with a sly grin. "I'm giving everyone a good laugh!"

Glitter sighed. "One day, Tumble, you're going to realize that Christmas is more than just fun and games."

Tumble just shrugged and twirled a shiny ribbon around his finger, already plotting his next prank.

The workshop was at its busiest. Christmas was only a few days away, and every elf was working around the clock to make sure everything was perfect. The sound of hammers, saws, and jingling bells filled the air. Santa's Naughty and Nice List was being checked for the final time, and the reindeer were getting in shape for their big night.

Tumble, however, was up to no good again. This time, he had decided to switch the labels on Santa's gift sacks. He swapped the ones marked "Nice" with those marked "Naughty," giggling at the chaos it would cause on Christmas morning.

"Just imagine," he chuckled to himself, "all the nice kids getting coal and the naughty ones getting toys! It'll be the greatest prank ever!"

But as Tumble was tying the last knot, a voice boomed behind him.

"What's going on here?"

Tumble spun around to see Bernard, the head elf, staring at him with crossed arms and a frown as stern as Santa's when the milk is sour.

"I... I was just organizing the sacks!" Tumble stammered, trying to hide the mischievous twinkle in his eye.

"Organizing, huh?" Bernard said, raising an eyebrow. "Then you won't mind if I check your work."

Before Tumble could stop him, Bernard yanked one of the sacks open. Out spilled a pile of coal, right onto the floor.

"Tumble!" Bernard roared. "Do you realize what you've done? If Santa had delivered these bags by mistake, it would have ruined Christmas!"

Tumble shifted uncomfortably, his usual confidence replaced by guilt. "I didn't mean to ruin anything," he muttered.

Bernard sighed. "Pranks might be fun for you, but Christmas isn't about tricks and laughter at someone else's expense. It's about giving joy to others. Since you don't seem to understand that, I'm giving you a new assignment."

Tumble's ears perked up. "A new assignment?"

"Yes," Bernard said. "You're going to help Santa personally deliver gifts this year. Maybe then, you'll learn what Christmas is really about."

Tumble wasn't sure what to expect when he climbed onto Santa's sleigh that night. He had never left the workshop before, and the idea of flying through the skies filled him with both excitement and nervousness.

As the sleigh soared into the starry sky, Tumble watched in awe as the North Pole disappeared below them. The twinkling lights of towns and cities came into view, and Santa began landing on rooftops, delivering gifts with his sack slung over one shoulder.

"Tumble," Santa said after a while, "why don't you come help me with this next house?"

Tumble hesitated but nodded, following Santa down the chimney of a cozy little home. Inside, the Christmas tree sparkled with lights, and stockings were hung neatly by the fireplace. Santa quietly placed gifts under the tree, then turned to Tumble.

"Why don't you add the finishing touch?" Santa said, handing him a small wrapped package.

Tumble tiptoed over and placed the gift in front of the tree. As he did, he noticed a handwritten note on the mantle:

"Dear Santa, thank you for bringing us presents every year. This Christmas, all I want is for my little brother to be happy. He's been sick for a long time, but he loves trains. If you could bring him one, it would mean the world to him. Love, Mia."

Tumble felt a strange warmth in his chest as he read the note. He looked at the gift he had just placed under the tree and saw that it was a bright red toy train.

Back in the sleigh, Tumble couldn't stop thinking about the note. "Santa," he asked quietly, "do you read all the letters the children send you?"

"Every single one," Santa replied with a kind smile. "Every child has a wish, and it's my job to make sure they feel loved and remembered, no matter how big or small their request is."

Tumble was quiet for the rest of the night, helping Santa deliver gifts and seeing the joy that his work brought to children all over the world.

By the time they returned to the North Pole, Tumble's usual mischief had been replaced with a newfound sense of purpose. The next day, he went straight to Bernard and apologized.

"I get it now," Tumble said earnestly. "Christmas isn't about jokes or tricks. It's about making people happy."

Bernard nodded. "That's a lesson every elf needs to learn. I hope you'll remember it from now on."

"I will," Tumble promised.

And he did. From that day forward, Tumble became one of the hardest-working elves in the workshop. He still loved to laugh and have fun, but now he used his energy to spread joy instead of chaos.

As for Santa, he never forgot the change he saw in Tumble that Christmas Eve. Every year, when the season grew busy, he made sure to remind the other elves that even the naughtiest among them could learn the true spirit of Christmas.

And in the North Pole, Tumble's transformation became a story of its own—a tale about the power of kindness, redemption, and the magic of Christmas.

The End

Chapter 5: The Heart of Christmas

The soft glow of the snow globe surrounded Emma and Jack as they landed gently in the center of a sparkling village square. Around them, the Christmas Wonderland was alive with joy and celebration. Twinkling lights adorned every tree and lamppost, and snowflakes fell gently from a sky that seemed to shimmer with its own light. Children laughed as they built snowmen, and carolers sang in perfect harmony by the glow of a crackling fire.

"Look, Jack!" Emma said, pointing toward a grand clock tower at the edge of the square. "That must be the center of the village."

"Let's go!" Jack replied, grabbing Emma's hand as they trudged through the fresh snow.

As they neared the tower, a group of elves approached them. They were dressed in colorful outfits with jingling bells on their hats and boots. The leader, a cheerful elf with rosy cheeks, smiled warmly.

"Welcome, travellers!" he said with a bow. "We've been expecting you."

"Expecting us?" Emma asked, surprised.

"Of course!" the elf replied. "Every visitor who arrives through the snow globe has a purpose. The magic brought you here for a reason."

The children exchanged curious glances. What purpose could they have in this magical place?

The elf led them into the grand clock tower, where the room glowed with golden light. At the center of the room was a massive snow globe, larger and more intricate than Grandpa's. Inside it was a miniature version of the village, but something seemed off—while the village they had seen was bustling with life and joy, the scene inside the snow globe was dim and still.

"What happened to it?" Jack asked, his voice full of concern.

"This is the Heart of Christmas," the elf explained. "Its magic keeps our world alive and full of joy. But recently, the magic has begun to fade. We believe it's because people outside have started forgetting the true meaning of Christmas."

Emma felt a pang of sadness. She remembered how distracted her family had been before they were transported here—too busy with shopping lists and holiday stress to enjoy the season.

"How can we help?" she asked.

The elf smiled. "That's the spirit! To restore the Heart of Christmas, you must complete three tasks. Each task will remind you—and others—of what makes this season so special."

The first task took them to a cozy little cottage on the outskirts of the village. Inside, they found an elderly woman sitting by the fire, looking lonely and lost in thought. The elf explained that she had been alone for many Christmases and had forgotten what it felt like to celebrate.

Emma and Jack worked together to decorate her cottage, hanging ornaments on a tiny tree and placing a plate of cookies by the fire. Jack even taught the woman a silly song they used to sing with Grandpa. By the end of the evening, the woman was laughing and smiling, her joy lighting up the room.

The second task led them to a frozen lake where a group of children sat on the shore, looking enviously at the skaters on the ice. "They can't afford skates," the elf whispered.

Emma and Jack didn't hesitate. They ran back to the village and collected spare skates from the shops and homes, bringing them back to the children. Soon, the lake was filled with laughter as everyone skated together, creating a scene of joy and unity.

For the final task, the elf brought them to a large tree in the center of the village square. "This is the Giving Tree," he said. "It needs one final decoration—a symbol of love and family."

Emma reached into her pocket and pulled out a small photo of her and Jack with their grandfather. She had brought it with her when they first entered the snow globe. "This is perfect," she said softly.

Jack nodded, and together, they placed the photo on the tree. As they stepped back, the tree lit up with a golden glow, and the entire village erupted in cheers. The Heart of Christmas inside the clock tower sparkled to life, its magic restored.

Back in the tower, the elf smiled at them. "You've done it. The Heart of Christmas is alive again, thanks to you. And now, it's time for you to return home."

Emma and Jack felt a wave of bittersweet emotion as they stepped back into the swirling light of the snow globe. When they opened their eyes, they were back in Grandpa's living room, the snow globe still glowing faintly in their hands.

Their parents were there, looking worried but relieved. "Where have you been?" their mother asked.

Emma and Jack smiled at each other. "We were just learning what Christmas is all about," Jack said.

That evening, their family sat together, sharing stories and laughter by the fire. For the first time in a long time, the house was filled with the true spirit of Christmas. And on the mantle, Grandpa's snow globe shimmered, a silent reminder of the magical adventure that had brought them closer than ever before.

The End

Chapter 6: The Midnight Chime

The square was bathed in a silver glow as the townspeople gathered around the towering Christmas Clock. Its intricate golden gears shimmered in the moonlight, and its hands ticked closer to midnight. Emma and Liam stood at the edge of the crowd, their breath visible in the icy air, their hearts pounding with anticipation.

The mysterious clock had been silent for years, a beautiful but forgotten relic of the past. But tonight, something felt different. The air seemed charged with a magical energy, and the clock's face glowed faintly, as if it were waking up after a long slumber.

"Do you think it will really chime?" Liam whispered to Emma.

Emma nodded, clutching the ancient key in her mittened hand. "It has to. We've come too far for it not to work."

All eyes were on the clock as Emma stepped forward, the crowd parting to let her through. With a deep breath, she inserted the key into the hidden slot near the base of the clock. As she turned it, a soft hum filled the air, and the clock began to vibrate ever so slightly.

The hands moved closer and closer to midnight.

With each tick, the hum grew louder, turning into a melodic vibration that resonated through the square. The townspeople held their breath as the final seconds of Christmas Eve ticked away. When the clock struck twelve, a deep, rich chime echoed through the town, filling the air with a sound so beautiful it brought tears to Emma's eyes.

But the magic didn't stop there. As the chime rang out, golden sparks burst from the clock, drifting like fireflies into the night sky. The snow around the square sparkled, and a warm, glowing light spread through the crowd, wrapping everyone in a blanket of joy and wonder.

"It's working!" Liam shouted, his face alight with amazement.

The golden sparks danced through the air, landing gently on each person in the crowd. Wherever they touched, smiles appeared, old grudges faded, and a sense of togetherness filled the square. It was as if the clock had unlocked not just the magic of Christmas, but the spirit of love and kindness hidden in every heart.

For the first time in years, the town was alive with laughter and cheer. Strangers hugged, children danced, and families reunited. Emma and Liam stood together, their mission complete, their hearts full.

"It's beautiful," Emma said softly, watching the sparks fade into the night.

"It's more than that," Liam replied. "It's Christmas."

The clock struck twelve one last time, its golden glow slowly dimming. Though the chimes faded, the warmth and magic lingered, a gift to the town that would last long after Christmas morning.

As Emma and Liam walked home through the softly falling snow, they knew they had witnessed something extraordinary. The Christmas Clock had not just chimed—it had reminded everyone of the true magic of the season.

The End

Chapter 7: The Talking Christmas Tree

The Johnson family Christmas tree stood proudly in the corner of the living room, its branches draped in tinsel, twinkling lights, and ornaments collected over the years. Eight-year-old Max stared at it in awe as he added the finishing touch: a gold star that his mother handed him with a smile.

"Perfect," she said, stepping back to admire the tree. "It's like something out of a holiday card."

Max nodded, feeling a sense of pride. He loved Christmas—the music, the cookies, the magic. But this year, something felt different about the tree. He couldn't quite put his finger on it, but he felt as though the tree was... watching him.

Late that night, long after his parents had gone to bed, Max crept into the living room. The only light came from the soft glow of the tree, casting colorful shadows across the walls. He sat cross-legged on the floor, staring up at its twinkling branches.

"Why do you look so different this year?" he whispered, not expecting an answer.

To his shock, the tree's lights flickered, and a deep, cheerful voice rumbled from its branches. "Because I'm not just any tree, Max. I'm your tree."

Max jumped back, his eyes wide. "Y-you can talk?"

"Of course I can talk!" the tree replied with a chuckle. "But only to those who believe in Christmas magic."

Max stared at the tree in amazement. "This is impossible... but also really cool."

"I'll take that as a compliment," said the tree, its ornaments jingling softly. "Now, tell me, Max—why are you awake so late? Shouldn't you be dreaming about sugarplums and reindeer?"

Max hesitated. "I guess I wanted to be here... in case Santa came early."

The tree's lights twinkled brighter. "Ah, I see. But Max, Christmas isn't just about waiting for Santa. It's about something much bigger."

Max frowned. "What do you mean?"

The tree's branches rustled gently. "Let me show you."

Before Max could reply, the room began to change. The walls faded away, replaced by a starry night sky. Snow fell softly around him, and the tree stood beside him in a snowy forest, its lights glowing warmly.

"W-where are we?" Max stammered.

"This is where I come from," the tree said. "The magical forest where Christmas trees grow."

Max looked around in awe. Dozens of trees stood in neat rows, their branches glittering with ice and snow. But unlike his tree, these trees weren't decorated. They stood quietly, their bare branches reaching toward the sky.

"These trees look so... plain," Max said.

"They're waiting for their moment," the tree explained. "Each Christmas tree has a purpose. Some bring joy to families like yours. Others light up town squares or schools. But they all share the same job: to spread the magic of Christmas."

Max tilted his head. "But how do they spread magic? They're just trees."

The tree chuckled. "Magic isn't about what you see, Max. It's about what you feel. Let me show you something else."

The snowy forest dissolved, and Max found himself in a cozy living room. A little girl sat on the floor, gazing up at a scraggly, uneven Christmas tree that looked like it had been pieced together from leftovers. Its decorations were mismatched, and its lights flickered unevenly. Yet the girl's face was lit with pure joy as she placed a paper star at the top.

"Why is she so happy?" Max asked. "Her tree doesn't even look good."

"Because to her, it's not about how it looks," the tree said softly. "That tree was a gift from her older brother, who worked extra hours to buy it. It's not about the tree—it's about the love behind it."

Max watched as the girl ran to hug her brother, her laughter filling the room. For the first time, he began to understand what the tree meant.

The scene shifted again, and Max found himself standing in a hospital room. A boy around his age lay in bed, looking pale and tired. Beside him stood a small potted Christmas tree, its branches decorated with handmade ornaments and paper chains.

"Who brought him that tree?" Max asked.

"His classmates," the tree replied. "They wanted him to feel included, even though he couldn't be home for Christmas."

Max's heart swelled as he watched the boy's face light up. Even though he was stuck in the hospital, the little tree brought him a spark of joy.

Finally, the scene changed once more, and Max found himself back in his own living room. He looked at his tree, its ornaments twinkling brightly, and felt a newfound appreciation for everything it represented.

"You see, Max," the tree said gently, "Christmas magic isn't about the biggest presents or the fanciest decorations. It's about kindness, love, and the memories we create with the people we care about."

Max nodded slowly. "I think I get it now."

"Good," the tree said, its lights glowing warmly. "Now, it's time for you to go back to bed. Tomorrow is Christmas, after all."

When Max woke the next morning, he rushed to the living room. The tree stood quietly in its corner, looking as ordinary as ever. For a moment, Max wondered if it had all been a dream.

But then he noticed something new: a small paper ornament hanging on one of the branches. It wasn't there before, and it had a simple message written in golden letters:

"The greatest gift of Christmas is in your heart."

Smiling, Max reached out to touch the ornament. "Merry Christmas," he whispered to the tree.

And for just a moment, he thought he saw its lights twinkle in reply.

The End

Chapter 8: The Magic Candy Cane

The snow fell gently over Maplewood, a small town where Christmas seemed to glow a little brighter each year. In a cozy little house near the center of town, ten-year-old Sophie and her younger brother Alex were busy decorating the tree with their mother. They hung ornaments, strung lights, and placed candy canes on the branches, their laughter filling the room.

As Sophie reached into the box of decorations, her fingers brushed against something unusual. She pulled out a single candy cane, wrapped in shiny gold and silver foil, its red and white stripes glistening as though it was glowing from within.

"Where did this come from?" Sophie asked, holding up the candy cane.

Her mother paused and frowned. "I don't know. I don't remember buying that one."

"It's probably just a fancy one from the store," Alex said, grabbing it from Sophie's hand. "Can I eat it?"

Before their mother could answer, a soft voice filled the room.

"Careful, young one," the candy cane said.

Sophie and Alex froze. "Did... did that candy cane just talk?" Sophie whispered.

"Yes, I did," the candy cane replied, its voice smooth and melodic. "I'm not an ordinary candy cane. I'm a magic one."

Alex's eyes went wide. "A magic candy cane? What does that mean?"

"It means," the candy cane said, "that I can grant you three wishes. But use them wisely—magic works best when it's used for good."

Sophie and Alex exchanged astonished looks. Their mother, who hadn't heard the candy cane's voice, had already moved to the kitchen to bake cookies.

"This is incredible," Alex said, clutching the candy cane. "What should we wish for?"

"I don't know," Sophie said, biting her lip. "We should think about it first. The candy cane said we have to use the wishes wisely."

Alex nodded reluctantly. "Okay, but let's not take too long. What if it stops working?"

The candy cane chuckled softly. "Don't worry, little one. My magic is timeless."

For the rest of the evening, Sophie and Alex whispered about their wishes, imagining all the things they could ask for. But as they sat by the fire, Sophie noticed something. Their mother was humming a carol, but her eyes looked tired, and there was a faint shadow of worry on her face.

Sophie leaned closer to Alex. "Do you think we could use one of the wishes to help Mom?"

Alex frowned. "Help her how?"

"I don't know," Sophie said. "But she's been working so hard, and I think she could use something to make her happy."

Alex thought about it for a moment and then nodded. "Okay. Let's wish for her to have the best Christmas ever."

Sophie held the candy cane in both hands. "We wish for Mom to have the best Christmas ever."

The candy cane sparkled brightly, and a soft warmth filled the room. A moment later, the sound of the doorbell echoed through the house.

Their mother opened the door to find a group of neighbours standing outside, holding trays of food, gifts, and warm blankets. "We just wanted to stop by and say thank you for all you've done for the community this year," one of them said. "Merry Christmas!"

Their mother's eyes filled with tears of gratitude as she invited them inside. For the first time in weeks, Sophie saw her mother's face light up with pure joy.

That night, as Sophie and Alex lay in bed, Alex whispered, "That was amazing. What should we wish for next?"

Sophie thought about it. "Maybe something for the town. Remember how Dad used to talk about fixing the Christmas lights in the park? They haven't worked in years."

Alex nodded eagerly. "Let's do it! The park looks so sad without lights."

The next morning, the siblings took the candy cane to the park, where the bare trees stood in silence, their branches heavy with snow. Holding the candy cane together, they made their second wish.

"We wish for the park to be full of Christmas lights."

The candy cane glowed brightly, and within seconds, the park transformed. Strings of lights wrapped around every tree, glowing in shades of red, green, blue, and gold. A large Christmas tree appeared in the center, its star twinkling at the top. As word spread, families began arriving, their laughter and cheer filling the park once more.

"This is amazing," Alex said, his face glowing with excitement. "The whole town is happy again."

Sophie smiled, but her thoughts were already on their final wish. What could they do to make it truly special?

That evening, as they sat by the fire with the candy cane resting between them, Alex spoke up. "Sophie, can I make the last wish?"

"What do you want to wish for?" Sophie asked.

Alex hesitated. "I miss Dad. I wish he could be here for Christmas."

Sophie's heart ached. Their father had been deployed overseas for months, and while he sent letters and video messages, it wasn't the same as having him home.

"I miss him too," Sophie said softly. "But the candy cane's magic can't change everything. We have to be careful."

Alex nodded, his eyes watering. "I know. But maybe we can wish for something that feels like he's here."

Sophie thought about it and smiled. "I have an idea."

She held the candy cane tightly and whispered, "We wish for something that will bring our family closer together this Christmas."

The candy cane sparkled one last time, its light filling the room. When it faded, there was a knock at the door.

Their mother opened it to reveal a man in a red coat and a large white beard. "Ho, ho, ho!" he said. "Merry Christmas!"

"Santa?" Alex whispered, his eyes wide.

Santa stepped inside, carrying a large bag. "I heard there's a family here in need of a little extra Christmas cheer."

He sat with them by the fire, telling stories and sharing laughter. From his bag, he pulled out a special gift—a scrapbook filled with photos and letters from their father. As they flipped through the pages, Sophie and Alex felt as though their dad was right there with them.

"This is the best Christmas ever," Alex said, snuggling close to his sister.

Sophie looked at the candy cane, now resting quietly on the mantle. Its magic had brought joy, love, and togetherness to their family—and she knew she would never forget the lessons it had taught her.

As the snow fell gently outside, Sophie smiled and whispered, "Thank you."

The candy cane twinkled faintly, as if to say, You're welcome.

The End

Chapter 9: The North Pole Adventure

It was Christmas Eve, and siblings Ellie and Max were full of excitement. Their stockings were hung, the tree was twinkling, and they had just set out milk and cookies for Santa. But as much as their parents told them to go to bed, Ellie and Max couldn't resist staying up to catch a glimpse of the man in red.

"Do you really think we'll see him?" Max whispered, peeking out from behind the couch.

Ellie grinned. "If we're quiet enough. Just don't eat the cookies this time."

Max blushed. "I was hungry last year."

Suddenly, the room filled with a faint jingling sound. The siblings froze. From the chimney came a soft whoosh, followed by a cloud of soot—and there he was. Santa, in all his jolly glory, brushing ash off his red coat.

"It's really him!" Ellie mouthed to Max, her eyes wide.

Before they could say a word, Santa walked to the tree and began placing gifts under it. But as he turned to leave, he glanced back at the plate of cookies.

"Classic chocolate chip," he said with a chuckle, popping one into his mouth. "Perfect for the trip back."

As Santa turned toward the chimney, Max suddenly stood up. "Wait!"

Ellie tried to grab him, but it was too late. Santa spun around, his eyes twinkling with surprise.

"Well, hello there," Santa said warmly. "Shouldn't you two be in bed?"

"We just wanted to see you," Max stammered.

Santa chuckled. "Well, now you have. But it's time for me to go—lots of houses to visit, you know."

Ellie, determined not to miss out on the moment, spoke up. "Can we come with you? Just for a little bit?"

Santa raised an eyebrow, then smiled. "I suppose a short visit wouldn't hurt. But you'll have to be quick!"

Before they could think twice, Santa snapped his fingers, and they were outside on the roof, standing beside his gleaming sleigh. Eight reindeer snorted and pawed the snowy tiles, their bells jingling softly.

"Hop in!" Santa said, climbing into the driver's seat.

Ellie and Max scrambled into the sleigh, their hearts pounding with excitement. Santa flicked the reins, and with a magical jolt, the sleigh soared into the sky.

The ride was unlike anything Ellie and Max had ever experienced. The sleigh cut through the frosty night air, the stars close enough to touch. Towns and cities sparkled below like a sea of Christmas lights.

"Where are we going first?" Max asked, gripping the edge of the sleigh.

Santa smiled. "Not where—when. We're going to the North Pole before I finish my deliveries."

"The North Pole?" Ellie gasped.

"You'll love it," Santa said. "Hold tight!"

The sleigh picked up speed, and within moments, they were surrounded by a breathtaking expanse of snow and ice. In the distance, twinkling lights and towering candy-striped poles marked the entrance to Santa's village.

As they landed in the heart of the North Pole, Ellie and Max were overwhelmed by the sight. Elves bustled around the snowy streets, carrying armfuls of gifts and decorations. Gingerbread houses lined the roads, their candy windows glowing with warm light. In the center of it all stood a massive workshop, its chimneys puffing out steam and smoke.

"This is incredible," Ellie whispered.

"Welcome to my home," Santa said with a grin, hopping out of the sleigh. "Come on—I'll show you around."

The siblings followed Santa through the bustling village. Inside the workshop, conveyor belts carried toys of every kind, and elves worked diligently at stations, hammering, painting, and wrapping.

"This is where the magic happens," Santa explained. "Everything you've ever dreamed of under the tree starts right here."

An elf approached Santa, holding a clipboard. "The final batch is ready, sir."

"Perfect timing," Santa said. Turning to Ellie and Max, he added, "Would you like to help?"

"Really?" Max asked, his face lighting up.

Santa handed them each a small gift. "Place these in the sleigh, and we'll be on our way."

As they helped load the sleigh, Ellie noticed a small, sad-looking elf sitting on a nearby bench. His pointed hat drooped, and he sighed as he watched the hustle and bustle around him.

"Is he okay?" Ellie asked Santa.

Santa followed her gaze and smiled gently. "That's Pip. He's one of our newest elves and hasn't quite found his place yet. Maybe you two can cheer him up."

Ellie and Max approached Pip. "Hi," Ellie said kindly. "Why aren't you helping?"

Pip sighed. "I tried, but I keep messing up. I painted a fire truck purple by mistake, and I wrapped a teddy bear in the wrong paper. Now I'm just in the way."

Max grinned. "I'm terrible at wrapping too. Once, I used duct tape instead of ribbon."

Ellie laughed. "Yeah, and he ate half the cookies we left for Santa last year."

Pip blinked, then chuckled softly. "You're not perfect either?"

“Not even close,” Ellie said. “But Christmas isn’t about being perfect. It’s about trying your best and spreading joy.”

Pip’s face brightened. “You’re right. Maybe I can help again.”

“Of course you can,” Max said. “Come on—Santa’s waiting.”

Pip joined them as they finished loading the sleigh. With the last gift in place, Santa turned to Ellie and Max. “You’ve done a wonderful job tonight. But it’s time for me to finish my deliveries—and time for you to head home.”

The siblings’ faces fell. “Do we have to?” Max asked.

Santa chuckled. “You’ve had quite the adventure, but there are families waiting for you. Besides, Christmas morning is just around the corner.”

With a snap of his fingers, Santa whisked them back into the sleigh. As they soared through the night sky once more, the North Pole disappeared into the distance, its lights twinkling like stars.

When Ellie and Max woke up the next morning, they were back in their living room. The tree sparkled with lights, and their stockings were filled to the brim. For a moment, they wondered if it had all been a dream.

But then Max spotted something on the mantle—a tiny elf hat, folded neatly next to a note. The note read:

“Thank you for helping us. Merry Christmas! Love, Pip.”

Ellie and Max exchanged smiles, their hearts full of wonder. They knew that this Christmas was one they’d never forget—a magical adventure that had shown them the true spirit of the season.

The End

Chapter 10: The Frozen Kingdom

Snow fell steadily as Lucy wandered through the dense forest, her boots crunching on the frosty ground. It was Christmas Eve, and the world around her seemed unusually quiet. The soft snow muffled every sound, leaving only the distant rustle of the wind. Lucy tugged her scarf tighter around her neck and paused to catch her breath, gazing at the towering pine trees that surrounded her.

"Why did I agree to get the firewood?" she muttered to herself, glancing at the empty sled she dragged behind her.

She had ventured deeper into the woods than she ever had before. As she bent down to gather a few sticks of kindling, a sudden shimmer caught her eye. A faint, glowing light flickered between the trees, its bluish hue dancing like the northern lights.

Curiosity bubbled up inside her. "What is that?" she whispered. Forgetting the firewood, Lucy stepped off the familiar path and followed the light. The deeper she ventured, the brighter it grew, until she came to a clearing unlike anything she had ever seen.

At the center of the clearing stood a massive archway made of ice, its surface sparkling like diamonds in the moonlight. Intricate carvings of snowflakes and stars decorated its edges, and through it, Lucy could see a world of white and blue—a kingdom made entirely of snow and ice.

She hesitated for only a moment before stepping through.

The air in the kingdom was crisp and cold, yet it didn't sting her skin the way winter air usually did. The snow beneath her feet was soft, glowing faintly as though lit from within. Surrounding her were towering ice castles, crystalline spires that shimmered under a pale, enchanted sky. Everywhere she looked, snowflakes danced lazily, suspended in the air as if time had slowed.

"This is amazing," Lucy breathed.

But the kingdom wasn't silent. The faint hum of voices carried through the stillness, and Lucy followed the sound. Soon, she found herself in the heart of the frozen city, where crowds of people—some human, some creatures she had never seen before—bustled about in hushed urgency. There were shimmering ice wolves, sparkling snow owls, and even small, glowing snowmen that waddled alongside their owners.

At the center of it all stood a tall woman in a flowing gown of white and silver, her hair cascading in waves of frost. A delicate crown of icicles adorned her head. She stood atop a platform, addressing the crowd with a voice that carried like the wind.

"Christmas is in jeopardy," the woman said, her tone heavy with worry. "The magic that powers our kingdom is fading, and with it, the spirit of Christmas. Without the Star of Winter, we cannot sustain the magic or the holiday."

Lucy stepped closer, her heart racing. Something about the woman's presence felt commanding yet kind. One of the glowing snowmen noticed Lucy and waddled up to her, squeaking excitedly.

"Who are you?" the queen asked, her gaze falling on Lucy. Despite the weight of her words, her expression softened.

"I'm Lucy," she said, her voice trembling slightly. "I don't know how I got here, but I heard what you said. What's happening to your kingdom?"

The queen sighed. "This is the Frozen Kingdom, the heart of winter and the magic of Christmas. Our power comes from the Star of Winter, a crystal that channels the joy and love of the season. But the star has been stolen."

"Stolen?" Lucy asked, horrified. "By who?"

"We don't know," the queen admitted. "All we know is that the magic is fading quickly. If we don't recover the star by midnight, not only will our kingdom crumble, but the spirit of Christmas will be lost to the world."

Lucy's heart ached. She thought of her family back home, their house filled with laughter and light. The idea of Christmas disappearing forever was unthinkable.

"I'll help you," she said firmly.

The queen's eyes widened in surprise. "You would do that?"

Lucy nodded. "I don't know much about magic, but I'll do whatever I can to save Christmas."

The queen smiled, and the air around her seemed to warm slightly. "Thank you, Lucy. Your courage gives me hope."

The queen led Lucy to a shimmering ice sled pulled by two majestic reindeer with silver antlers. "The star's light leaves a faint trail," the queen explained as they climbed aboard. "We'll follow it as far as we can."

As the sled raced through the frozen wilderness, Lucy couldn't help but marvel at the beauty of the kingdom. The ice-covered trees sparkled like chandeliers, and frozen rivers snaked through the landscape like silver ribbons. But the farther they travelled, the darker the sky became, and the glowing snow began to dim.

"There," the queen said, pointing ahead. A faint glimmer of blue light flickered in the distance, leading them to the mouth of a dark cave.

Lucy hesitated as the sled came to a stop. "What's in there?"

"Trouble," the queen said grimly. "This cave belongs to the Frost Wraiths, creatures that thrive on stealing joy and spreading despair. They must have taken the star."

Lucy swallowed hard. "How do we get it back?"

"Frost Wraiths are drawn to fear," the queen said. "But they cannot stand the warmth of hope or the light of joy. Remember that, Lucy."

The cave was cold and silent, its icy walls glowing faintly in the dark. As Lucy and the queen ventured deeper, eerie whispers filled the air, sending shivers down Lucy's spine.

In the center of the cavern, a group of shadowy figures loomed around a pedestal made of jagged ice. On the pedestal sat the Star of Winter, its light flickering weakly.

"Who dares enter our domain?" one of the Frost Wraiths hissed, its voice like cracking ice.

The queen stepped forward. "Return the star. It does not belong to you."

The wraiths laughed, their forms shifting like smoke. "The star's magic is ours now. Christmas will wither, and the Frozen Kingdom will fall."

Lucy's heart pounded. She felt the weight of the wraiths' dark presence pressing down on her, filling her with doubt. But then she remembered the queen's words: They cannot stand the warmth of hope or the light of joy.

Taking a deep breath, Lucy stepped forward. "You're wrong," she said, her voice trembling but firm. "Christmas isn't about fear or despair. It's about love and kindness, and that's something you can never take away."

The wraiths hissed and recoiled, their shadows flickering.

Lucy reached into her pocket and pulled out a small locket her mother had given her. Inside was a photo of her family, smiling together around the Christmas tree. She held it high, letting the memory fill her with warmth.

"This is what Christmas means to me," she said. "And no matter what you do, you can't take it away."

The light from the locket grew brighter, filling the cavern with a golden glow. The wraiths shrieked and began to dissolve, their shadows melting like frost in the sun.

The queen smiled proudly as she stepped forward and retrieved the Star of Winter. Its light grew stronger, and the cavern trembled as the magic of the Frozen Kingdom surged back to life.

Outside the cave, the sky was brighter, the snow glowing once more. The queen placed the star in the sled, and they raced back to the kingdom. When they arrived, cheers erupted from the crowd as the queen raised the restored star high above her head.

"Thanks to Lucy, Christmas is safe," the queen announced. "The Star of Winter shines once more!"

Lucy blushed as the crowd cheered for her, but her heart swelled with pride.

When it was time for Lucy to return home, the queen placed a hand on her shoulder. "You have a brave heart, Lucy. The magic of Christmas lives in you."

As the queen waved her hand, the shimmering archway appeared once more. Lucy stepped through and found herself back in the forest, her sled still empty but her heart full.

When she returned home, her family greeted her with hugs and laughter. And as she sat by the fire that evening, she glanced out the window, where a single star twinkled brightly in the night sky.

Lucy smiled, knowing that the Frozen Kingdom—and Christmas—were safe.

The End

Chapter 11: A Gift for Santa

Eight-year-old Mia sat cross-legged on her bedroom floor, staring at the glitter-covered paper in front of her. Her crayons were scattered across the carpet, and she held a green crayon poised above the page. But no matter how hard she thought, she couldn't decide what to draw.

"Mia, are you still working on your letter to Santa?" her mom called from the hallway.

"Sort of!" Mia called back. She wasn't writing a letter asking for presents—she was trying to figure out what to give Santa.

Everyone always thought about what they wanted from Santa, but no one seemed to think about him. He worked so hard every year, flying around the world to make everyone happy. Didn't Santa deserve a gift too?

"I just don't know what he'd like," Mia muttered to herself.

Her dog, Max, wagged his tail and nudged her hand, knocking the crayon onto the floor.

"Not now, Max," Mia sighed. "I need to think!"

Max tilted his head as if to say, Maybe I can help.

The next day at school, Mia asked her friends for ideas. "What would you give Santa for Christmas?"

"Cookies," said Jason, shrugging. "Everyone gives him cookies."

"But that's boring," said Sophie. "I'd give him a new sleigh! Something faster and shinier."

"Yeah, but he probably already has the best sleigh," Mia said.

Her teacher, Mrs. Fields, overheard their conversation and smiled. "That's a very thoughtful idea, Mia. It's not about how big or fancy the gift is—it's about how much it means to the person you're giving it to."

Mia nodded thoughtfully. Maybe the best gift for Santa wasn't something bought or built. Maybe it was something from the heart.

That evening, Mia sat by the fireplace, watching the twinkling lights on the Christmas tree. Max curled up beside her, resting his head on her lap. As she scratched behind his ears, an idea began to form in her mind.

"What if..." she whispered, her face lighting up. "What if I made something special for him?"

Max wagged his tail as if to say, That's it!

Mia jumped up and ran to her craft box. She pulled out paper, markers, glue, and glitter, her mind racing with ideas. She stayed up late, cutting and colouring until her fingers were sticky and her room was covered in glitter.

When she was done, she held up her creation: a hand-drawn card shaped like Santa's sleigh. Inside, she wrote a simple message:

Dear Santa,

Thank you for all the joy you bring to the world. I hope this Christmas, you feel as loved and special as you make everyone else feel.

Love, Mia

She smiled, proud of her work. But something was missing. What else could she add to make it perfect?

On Christmas Eve, Mia had an idea. She opened her treasure box and pulled out her favorite snow globe. It was small, with a tiny Santa inside, surrounded by swirling glitter. Her grandpa had given it to her last year, saying it would always remind her of the magic of Christmas.

Mia hesitated for a moment. The snow globe was special to her. But that's what made it the perfect gift.

She carefully wrapped the snow globe and tucked it into her card. Then she placed the package under the tree, right next to the plate of cookies and milk.

"Do you think he'll like it, Max?" she asked.

Max wagged his tail, his eyes shining with approval.

That night, Mia had trouble falling asleep. She kept imagining Santa finding her gift. Would he smile? Would he be surprised? Finally, exhaustion took over, and she drifted off.

When she woke up the next morning, the first thing she did was race to the tree. The plate of cookies was empty, the milk glass was half full—and her gift was gone.

In its place was a small note written in elegant, swirling handwriting:

Dear Mia,

Thank you for the most thoughtful gift. It's rare that anyone thinks about giving me something, and your card and snow globe warmed my heart. You've reminded me why I love what I do.

Merry Christmas!

Love, Santa

Mia's heart swelled with joy. She hugged Max tightly, then showed the note to her parents, who smiled proudly.

That Christmas was the best one Mia had ever had—not because of the presents she received, but because she had found a way to give something truly meaningful.

And somewhere, far away in the North Pole, Santa placed Mia's snow globe on his desk, a reminder that even he was thought of and loved.

The End

Chapter 12: The Lonely Snowman

In the quiet corner of a snowy park, a snowman stood alone. He had been built weeks ago by a group of children who had laughed and played as they shaped him, giving him a carrot nose, shiny black buttons, and a scarf borrowed from someone's coat. But as the days passed, the children stopped coming.

Now, the snowman stood silently, watching the empty park. The laughter had faded, and the only sound was the rustling of the wind through the bare trees.

"I suppose they've forgotten me," the snowman said softly to himself. His voice, if anyone could hear it, would have sounded like the whisper of snowflakes falling on fresh powder. "I'm just a pile of snow now. No one needs me."

The snowman tried not to feel sad, but the long, quiet days made it hard not to. He spent his time gazing at the sky, wondering what it might feel like to have a purpose beyond standing still.

One evening, as the snowman stood lost in his thoughts, he noticed a small movement in the distance. A little girl in a red coat was struggling to pull a sled piled high with firewood through the deep snow. She stumbled, and the sled tipped, spilling the wood everywhere.

The snowman wanted to help, but he was rooted to the ground. Still, he called out softly, "Do you need help?"

The girl froze, her wide eyes scanning the empty park. "Who's there?" she whispered.

"It's me," the snowman said. "Over here."

The girl turned toward him, her face filled with surprise. "You can talk?"

"Yes," the snowman replied. "I may be just a snowman, but I'd like to help you if I can."

The girl hesitated, then smiled shyly. "I could use some help. This wood is too heavy for me to carry on my own."

The snowman thought for a moment. He couldn't move, but he could use what he had. "Bring the sled here," he said. "Pile the wood against me, and I'll hold it steady while you stack it neatly."

The girl did as he suggested, and together they managed to balance the load back onto the sled.

"Thank you, Mr. Snowman," the girl said, her cheeks pink from the cold. "You're not just standing here—you're helping me."

The snowman felt a flicker of happiness. "I'm glad I could help," he said. "What's your name?"

"Lila," the girl said. "I live just over the hill."

"It's nice to meet you, Lila," the snowman said.

Lila waved as she pulled the sled toward home, her red coat bright against the snowy landscape. The snowman watched her go, feeling a warmth in his heart that he hadn't felt in days.

The next morning, the snowman woke to find Lila standing in front of him again. This time, she had brought a group of children with her.

"This is the snowman I told you about!" Lila said, her voice full of excitement. "He's alive!"

The other children stared at him, their eyes wide. "Really?" one of them asked. "You can talk?"

"I can," the snowman said, his voice as soft as the falling snow. "It's nice to meet you all."

The children spent the day playing in the park, building snow forts and throwing snowballs. They included the snowman in their games, decorating him with a new scarf and an extra layer of buttons. For the first time in weeks, the snowman didn't feel forgotten. He felt like he belonged.

As the days went on, the snowman became the heart of the park. Children came to visit him every day, bringing him stories, snacks (which he couldn't eat but appreciated), and even a pair of mittens for his stick hands. He became a friend to everyone who passed by.

But one afternoon, Lila arrived with tears in her eyes.

"What's wrong, Lila?" the snowman asked gently.

"It's my friend Oliver," she said. "He's sick, and he can't leave his house to play in the snow."

The snowman thought for a moment. "Then we'll bring the snow to him," he said.

"But how?" Lila asked.

"Gather your friends," the snowman said. "Bring shovels and sleds. We'll build him his own snowman."

The children worked tirelessly, scooping snow into sleds and pulling it to Oliver's yard. They built a snowman even taller than the one in the park, decorating it with a top hat, a scarf, and a bright smile.

When Oliver looked out the window and saw the snowman, his face lit up. Lila waved at him, and Oliver waved back, his smile so big it made everyone's hearts feel warm.

"That's the magic of snowmen," the park snowman said softly to himself, watching from afar. "We may be made of snow, but we bring joy that's as warm as sunshine."

As the days grew longer and the snow began to melt, the snowman stood quietly in the park, content. He had helped Lila, played with the children, and even brought happiness to Oliver. He had found his purpose.

And though the sun grew warmer each day, the snowman didn't feel sad. He knew that even if he melted away, the joy he had brought to others would remain.

"I may just be a snowman," he said softly to himself, "but I've made a difference. And that's enough for me."

The End

Chapter 13: The Christmas Puppy

The snow fell steadily over the small town of Willow Creek, blanketing the streets and rooftops in a soft, glistening layer of white. In an empty alley behind a row of shops, a tiny, scruffy puppy huddled beneath an old cardboard box. His fur, once golden and shiny, was matted and dirty, and his small body shivered from the cold.

The puppy didn't have a name or a family. He had spent his short life wandering the streets, scavenging for scraps and curling up in dark corners to keep warm. But as Christmas approached, the town seemed brighter, and for the first time, the little puppy felt a flicker of hope.

"Maybe," he thought, curling his tail tightly around himself, "this Christmas, I'll find a family."

That same morning, eight-year-old Lily Parker was sitting by the window of her cozy living room, watching the snow fall. The Christmas tree sparkled behind her, and the smell of cookies baking filled the air, but Lily's heart felt heavy.

All she wanted for Christmas was a puppy. She had written it in her letter to Santa, asked her parents a hundred times, and even drawn pictures of what her puppy might look like. But her parents always gave the same answer.

"Maybe when you're older, Lily," her mom had said gently. "A puppy is a big responsibility."

Lily sighed and rested her chin on her knees. She didn't want to wait. She wanted a furry friend to love and care for now, someone to share her adventures and keep her company.

Later that day, as Lily and her mom walked to the market to pick up some last-minute ingredients, Lily spotted something unusual. In the alley behind the bakery, a small movement caught her eye. She stopped and squinted, trying to see through the falling snow.

"Mom, look!" Lily said, tugging at her mother's coat.

There, beneath a sagging cardboard box, was the scruffy little puppy. His dark eyes peeked out nervously, and he let out a tiny, pitiful whine.

"Oh, you poor thing," Lily whispered, kneeling down. The puppy flinched at first, but when she held out her hand, he sniffed it cautiously. His tail wagged just a little.

"Lily, don't get too close," her mom said, sounding concerned. "We don't know if he's safe."

"But, Mom," Lily pleaded, "he's just a baby! He's all alone. We have to help him."

Her mother hesitated, looking at the shivering puppy. Finally, she sighed. "All right. Let's take him to the vet first and make sure he's okay."

Lily's heart leapt with excitement. Carefully, she scooped up the puppy and wrapped him in her scarf. He snuggled into her warmth, his small body trembling less with every step they took.

At the vet's office, the puppy was given a clean bill of health, though he was underweight and needed some care. "He's lucky you found him," the vet said with a smile. "He wouldn't have lasted much longer in this cold."

Lily looked at her mom with wide, hopeful eyes. "Can we keep him? Please?"

Her mom knelt down, brushing a strand of hair from Lily's face. "Taking care of a puppy is a big job, Lily. Are you sure you're ready for it?"

"I'm sure," Lily said firmly. "I'll feed him, walk him, and make sure he's happy. I promise."

Her mom smiled softly. "All right. Let's bring him home."

Back at the house, the puppy explored his new surroundings cautiously. He sniffed the soft rug by the fireplace, wagged his tail at the twinkling Christmas tree, and let out a happy bark when Lily placed a bowl of food in front of him.

"You need a name," Lily said, sitting cross-legged on the floor as the puppy ate. She thought for a moment, watching his golden fur shine in the firelight. "How about Charlie? Do you like that?"

The puppy wagged his tail so hard he almost knocked over his bowl. Lily laughed. "Charlie it is."

Over the next few days, Charlie and Lily became inseparable. He followed her everywhere, his little paws clicking on the wooden floors. They played in the snow, chased each other around the yard, and cuddled by the fire every evening. For the first time in his life, Charlie felt safe and loved.

On Christmas morning, Charlie woke Lily by licking her face. She giggled and hugged him tightly, feeling like she'd received the best gift in the world.

As the Parker family opened presents around the tree, Charlie curled up in Lily's lap, his eyes bright with happiness. Her parents had even bought him a small red collar with a shiny tag that said, Charlie.

"Thank you, Santa," Lily whispered, stroking his soft fur.

That evening, as the snow fell softly outside, Lily sat by the window with Charlie in her arms. She thought about how lonely he must have been before they found him and how much joy he had already brought into their home.

"You're not just my Christmas gift, Charlie," she said, kissing the top of his head. "You're my best friend."

Charlie barked softly, as if to say, And you're my family.

From that day on, Charlie was never lonely again. And every Christmas, Lily would hang a special ornament on the tree—a small paw print with Charlie's name on it—to remind them of the year they found each other.

The End

Chapter 14: The Wish on the Star

It was Christmas Eve, and seven-year-old Ben sat at his bedroom window, staring up at the starry sky. Outside, the world was blanketed in snow, the soft glow of Christmas lights reflecting off the white. But inside Ben's house, it didn't feel like Christmas at all.

His mom was in the kitchen, too busy preparing dinner to hum carols like she used to. His dad was in his office, frowning at his laptop, muttering about deadlines. And his older sister Emma had locked herself in her room, glued to her phone.

Ben sighed. Christmas hadn't been the same since last year, when his family started arguing about everything—money, schedules, even who got to hang the star on the tree.

This year, there hadn't even been a star. Their Christmas tree stood in the corner, its top bare and its lights dull.

Ben pulled a blanket around his shoulders and looked up at the brightest star in the sky. It twinkled softly, almost like it was winking at him.

"I wish," Ben whispered, his breath fogging up the glass, "I wish my family could be happy again."

The star seemed to shine a little brighter, and for a moment, Ben thought he saw it move. He blinked, but the star was still there, twinkling like normal.

"Maybe stars don't grant wishes," he muttered. But as he crawled into bed, he couldn't shake the feeling that something magical might happen.

The next morning, Ben woke to the smell of cinnamon and pine. He rubbed his eyes and sat up. The house was quiet—too quiet.

When he wandered into the living room, he froze. The Christmas tree was glowing, its lights brighter than he had ever seen them. And at the very top, a star sparkled like it had been plucked straight from the sky.

"What's going on?" Ben whispered.

His mom appeared from the kitchen, her face glowing with a warm smile. "Good morning, sweetheart," she said. "Merry Christmas."

Ben blinked in surprise. His mom's voice sounded soft and happy—just like it used to.

Before he could ask about the star, his dad came in, carrying a tray of hot cocoa. He set it on the table and ruffled Ben's hair. "There you are, buddy. You're just in time for breakfast."

"Is... is everything okay?" Ben asked cautiously.

His dad frowned. "Of course it is. Why wouldn't it be?"

Ben didn't know what to say. This wasn't how Christmas had felt in years.

As the morning went on, more surprises followed. Emma came downstairs without her phone, laughing as she joined Ben in a snowball fight outside. Their parents watched from the porch, sipping cocoa and holding hands. Ben couldn't remember the last time they had done that.

After lunch, the whole family worked together to bake cookies, telling stories and singing carols while they waited for the oven timer to ding. For the first time in a long time, the house was filled with warmth and laughter.

That evening, as they sat around the fireplace, Ben's dad held up a box wrapped in golden paper. "This," he said, "is for all of us."

The family gathered around as he opened the box to reveal a simple wooden frame. Inside was a photo of them from years ago, before things had changed—smiling together around a Christmas tree.

Ben's mom teared up. "I remember that day," she said softly. "We were so happy."

Emma nodded. "Can we take a new family photo? Right now?"

Ben grinned as they set up the camera, arranging themselves in front of the glowing tree. When the timer went off, Ben looked at the photo on the screen and felt his heart swell. Everyone was smiling—really smiling.

That night, Ben returned to his bedroom window, looking up at the star that had seemed so bright the night before.

"Thank you," he whispered. "Thank you for making my wish come true."

The star twinkled in reply, and for a moment, Ben thought he saw it wink.

The End

Chapter 15: The Orphan's Christmas Angel

In the quiet corner of St. Mary's Orphanage, ten-year-old Clara sat by the frosted window, staring out at the snow-covered town below. The warm glow of Christmas lights twinkled in the distance, but inside Clara's heart, there was only coldness and sadness.

It was Christmas Eve, a time for joy and family, but Clara had neither. She had been at St. Mary's for as long as she could remember, moving from one foster home to another and always finding herself back here. The other children laughed and played, but Clara preferred to be alone, watching the snowflakes drift past the window.

"What's the point of Christmas?" she muttered to herself. "It's not like anyone cares about me."

A single tear rolled down her cheek as she turned away from the window. She didn't notice the faint shimmer of light that appeared outside.

That night, as Clara lay in bed, she heard a soft sound, like the rustling of wings. Sitting up, she blinked in the dim light of the dormitory. At the foot of her bed stood a figure wrapped in a glowing, golden light.

"Who... who are you?" Clara whispered, her voice trembling.

The figure stepped closer, revealing a kind face framed by soft, golden curls. She wore a flowing white gown, and her eyes sparkled like the stars.

"I'm Grace," the figure said, her voice warm and soothing. "I'm an angel, and I've come to help you."

"An angel?" Clara asked, her eyes wide. "Why would you come to see me?"

"Because," Grace said gently, "you made a wish. You wished for someone to care about you."

Clara looked down, her cheeks burning with embarrassment. "That's not something an angel can fix."

Grace knelt beside her, her glow illuminating the small bed. "Oh, Clara, you're wrong. Christmas is a time for miracles, and sometimes the greatest miracle is helping someone see the love that's already around them."

Clara frowned. "What do you mean?"

"Come with me," Grace said, holding out her hand. "I'll show you."

Before Clara could protest, Grace touched her hand, and the room faded away. In an instant, Clara found herself standing outside, the snow crunching beneath her feet. The orphanage glowed softly in the distance.

"Where are we?" Clara asked, shivering.

"This is your past," Grace said. "Come, let me show you something."

Grace led Clara to a small park just outside the town square. A group of children played in the snow, their laughter echoing in the frosty air. Among them, Clara saw a younger version of herself, building a snowman with a boy and a girl.

"Do you remember this day?" Grace asked.

Clara's heart ached with the memory. "That's Ellie and Sam," she said softly. "They were my foster siblings... before I came back to St. Mary's."

"They loved you," Grace said, her voice full of kindness. "And they still think about you. You left a mark on their hearts."

Clara's eyes filled with tears. "I thought they forgot about me."

"Love like that doesn't fade," Grace said. "But there's more to see."

With a wave of Grace's hand, the scene shifted. They were now inside St. Mary's dining hall, where the other children were gathered around a Christmas tree. Sister Margaret, the headmistress, stood at the front, handing out presents.

Clara spotted herself sitting in a corner, away from the group. But what caught her attention was Sister Margaret, who glanced at her younger self with a look of sadness.

"She always tried to make me feel special," Clara murmured, remembering the small treats and kind words Sister Margaret had given her over the years.

"She cares for you deeply," Grace said. "But sometimes, when we feel lonely, we don't see the love that's right in front of us."

Clara wiped her eyes. "I never said thank you."

"There's still time," Grace said with a smile.

They stood outside the orphanage, peering through the frosted windows. Inside, the other children were decorating the tree, their faces lit with joy. Sister Margaret was busy in the kitchen, baking cookies for the Christmas celebration.

But what caught Clara's attention was a small box sitting on the mantel. On the side was written, "For Clara."

"What's that?" Clara asked.

"It's a gift," Grace said. "From the other children. They've noticed how lonely you've been, and they wanted to make sure you felt included this Christmas."

Clara's heart swelled. "They... did that for me?"

"Yes," Grace said softly. "Even when you feel alone, there are people who care for you. You just have to let them in."

When Clara blinked, she was back in her bed at St. Mary's. The dormitory was quiet, and for a moment, she wondered if it had all been a dream. But when she looked out the window, she saw a soft golden glow in the sky—a reminder of Grace.

The next morning, Clara woke up with a sense of purpose. She joined the other children in the dining hall, smiling and laughing as they ate breakfast together. When Sister Margaret handed her the small box from the mantel, Clara opened it to find a handmade scarf, knitted in her favorite color.

"Thank you," Clara said, her voice trembling with emotion. "This means so much to me."

Sister Margaret hugged her tightly. "You're part of our family, Clara. Never forget that."

For the first time in years, Clara felt truly at home. And as she sat by the Christmas tree that evening, surrounded by warmth and laughter, she whispered a quiet thank-you to the angel who had shown her the way.

The End

Chapter 16: Santa's Bad Hair Day

It was Christmas Eve, and Santa was well into his yearly journey, delivering presents to children around the world. His sleigh soared through the frosty night sky, and the reindeer pulled it effortlessly. Santa hummed a cheerful tune as he checked his list for the next stop.

"Next up: the Greenfield house," Santa said to himself, steering the sleigh toward the quiet suburban neighbourhood below. The house was nestled at the end of the street, its windows glowing with soft, golden light.

Santa landed the sleigh on the roof with a gentle thud. He adjusted his red coat, grabbed his sack of toys, and approached the chimney. "Here we go," he muttered, swinging his legs over the edge. "Ho, ho, ho, and down I go!"

But as he slid into the chimney, something unexpected happened.

"Hmmph—what's this?" Santa muttered, wiggling his shoulders. His descent came to an abrupt halt as something tugged at his face. His beard had caught on a jagged brick inside the chimney.

"Oh no," Santa groaned, pulling at his beard. But the more he tugged, the tighter it seemed to stick. "Well, this is a fine pickle."

Santa wriggled and squirmed, but he couldn't budge. His normally jolly demeanour began to fade as frustration set in. He glanced down at his sack of toys, wedged just below him. "Can't let this ruin Christmas," he said firmly. "Think, Santa, think."

After a moment, Santa reached into his pocket and pulled out a small gadget that the elves had given him earlier that year—a "Chimney Unsticker 3000." It looked like a tiny can of spray. "Just in case," the elves had said.

"Well, now's as good a time as any," Santa muttered. He twisted the can's nozzle and aimed it at his beard. With a soft hiss, a fine mist sprayed over the tangled hairs. For a moment, nothing happened.

And then—

"Whoosh!"

The spray worked a little too well. Santa shot down the rest of the chimney like a cannonball, landing with a thud in the fireplace below. Soot puffed up in a cloud around him, coating his red suit in black dust.

"Perfect," Santa muttered, brushing himself off. "At least I made it down."

But as he stood up, he caught sight of his reflection in the glass of the fireplace screen. His beard, usually pristine and fluffy, was now a tangled, singed mess. One side stuck out at an odd angle, while the other drooped limply.

"Oh dear," Santa said, his cheeks turning redder than usual. "This won't do at all."

Determined not to let his bad hair day ruin Christmas, Santa got to work placing presents under the tree. But as he moved around the room, a soft giggle caught his attention.

Santa spun around to find a little girl standing in the doorway, her eyes wide with wonder. She held a stuffed rabbit tightly in one arm, and her other hand was pressed to her mouth, trying to stifle her laughter.

"Santa?" she whispered, her voice full of awe. "Is it really you?"

Santa straightened up, smoothing his coat. "Indeed it is," he said, his voice booming. But then he remembered his dishevelled appearance and tried to turn away, hoping she wouldn't notice.

The girl tilted her head. "What happened to your beard?"

Santa sighed. "Let's just say chimneys aren't always as smooth as they look."

The girl giggled again, stepping closer. "It looks... funny."

Santa chuckled, unable to stay embarrassed. "I suppose it does, doesn't it? But it's nothing a good brushing won't fix."

The girl's laughter grew, and soon Santa found himself laughing too. "What's your name, little one?" he asked.

"Ellie," she said, her eyes sparkling. "I can fix your beard if you want. My mom's a hairdresser, and she taught me how to brush out tangles."

Santa raised an eyebrow. "You'd help an old fellow like me?"

Ellie nodded eagerly. "Of course! But you have to promise not to leave before I get back."

Santa smiled warmly. "You have my word."

Ellie dashed off and returned moments later with a small brush and a bottle of detangling spray. She set to work, carefully brushing out Santa's beard while he sat on the floor by the tree. Santa hummed a Christmas carol as she worked, and Ellie couldn't help but sing along.

"There!" Ellie said proudly after a few minutes. Santa's beard was once again smooth and fluffy, gleaming white like freshly fallen snow.

"Perfect!" Santa said, standing up and admiring his reflection in an ornament. "You're quite the talented young lady, Ellie. Thank you."

Ellie beamed. "You're welcome, Santa. Will you tell the elves I helped you?"

Santa nodded. "Absolutely. I'll even put you on my helper list."

Ellie's eyes widened. "There's a helper list?"

"Oh yes," Santa said, his eyes twinkling. "It's for special children who go above and beyond to spread Christmas cheer."

Ellie hugged her stuffed rabbit tightly, her face glowing with joy.

Before Santa climbed back up the chimney, he reached into his sack and pulled out a beautifully wrapped gift. "This is for you, Ellie," he said. "A little extra thank-you for saving my Christmas look."

Ellie gasped. "Really? What is it?"

"Open it tomorrow," Santa said with a wink. "Christmas morning is always the best time for surprises."

Ellie nodded, her heart racing with excitement.

As Santa climbed back up the now-clear chimney, he called out, "Merry Christmas, Ellie! And thank you again!"

"Merry Christmas, Santa!" Ellie called back, waving until he disappeared.

As the sleigh soared into the sky, Santa's laugh echoed through the night. "Ho, ho, ho! Another adventure for the books. Now, Dasher, onward to the next house!"

And though he had faced one of the silliest mishaps of his career, Santa knew it had been worth it. Thanks to Ellie, his beard—and his Christmas spirit—were as bright as ever.

The End

Chapter 17: The Case of the Stolen Cookies

It was Christmas Eve at the Watson household, and everything was perfect. The tree sparkled with colorful lights, the stockings were hung by the fireplace, and the smell of freshly baked cookies filled the air. Emma and her little brother Ben had spent the afternoon making a batch of Santa's favorite chocolate chip cookies, leaving them on a festive plate with a tall glass of milk.

"Do you think Santa will eat all the cookies this year?" Ben asked, licking a bit of stray frosting off his finger.

"Of course he will," Emma replied confidently. "Santa loves cookies."

The siblings went to bed that night, their hearts full of excitement. But when Emma woke early the next morning, something was very wrong.

"Ben!" she whispered, shaking her brother awake. "The cookies are gone!"

Ben sat up, rubbing his eyes. "Isn't that the point? Santa—"

"No!" Emma interrupted. "The cookies are gone, but the milk is still there. Santa always drinks the milk."

Ben frowned. "So... if Santa didn't eat them, who did?"

Emma narrowed her eyes. "That's what we're going to find out."

The Investigation Begins

Emma and Ben crept into the living room, where the empty plate of cookies sat on the coffee table. The glass of milk was untouched, its surface as smooth as ice.

"This is strange," Emma muttered. "Santa wouldn't leave without drinking the milk. That means someone else must have eaten the cookies."

Ben's eyes widened. "You mean... there's a cookie thief?"

"Exactly," Emma said, grabbing a notepad and pencil. "We need to gather clues."

The siblings began their investigation, starting with the plate. Emma leaned in close, examining the crumbs left behind.

"Hmm," she said, scribbling in her notebook. "There are a lot of crumbs, but they're all on one side of the plate. Whoever ate the cookies must have been in a hurry."

Ben crouched by the table, sniffing the air. "I smell peanut butter!"

"Peanut butter?" Emma repeated. "We didn't make peanut butter cookies."

Ben nodded. "I think the thief had peanut butter breath."

Emma added the detail to her notes. "Good observation. Now let's look for footprints."

Clues in the Living Room

The siblings searched the floor around the coffee table. At first, they didn't see anything unusual, but then Ben pointed to a small, sticky spot near the edge of the rug.

"Look! It's a trail of frosting," Ben said.

Emma crouched down, following the trail with her eyes. It led from the coffee table toward the fireplace. As she approached, she spotted something unusual: a single black thread snagged on the edge of the rug.

"This could be important," Emma said, holding up the thread. "Do you think it belongs to the thief?"

Ben shrugged. "Maybe they were wearing black clothes."

Emma added the thread to her growing list of clues. "We need to keep looking."

Suspects in the House

The siblings decided to interview everyone in the house to see if they could find the culprit. First, they went to their parents' room.

"Mom, Dad," Emma said, waking them gently. "Did either of you eat the cookies we left for Santa?"

Their mom groaned sleepily. "No, honey. Why would we eat Santa's cookies?"

"Are you sure?" Ben asked, squinting suspiciously. "You do like chocolate chip cookies."

Their dad chuckled. "We promise it wasn't us. Check the kitchen—maybe the cookie jar has some answers."

Emma and Ben exchanged a glance and headed to the kitchen. There, they found Max, their golden retriever, lying on the floor with his head resting on his paws.

"Max!" Emma said, pointing an accusing finger. "Did you eat the cookies?"

Max wagged his tail but didn't move. Ben knelt beside him, sniffing his breath.

"No peanut butter," Ben declared. "I don't think it was Max."

Emma sighed. "Okay, so it's not Mom, Dad, or Max. Who else could it be?"

A Surprising Discovery

Just as they were about to give up, a faint noise caught their attention. It was coming from the hallway closet. Emma and Ben tiptoed toward the door, their hearts pounding. Emma slowly turned the knob and flung the door open.

There, crouched among the winter coats, was their older cousin Jake, holding the last cookie in his hand. His eyes widened in surprise, and crumbs fell from his mouth.

"Jake!" Emma shouted. "It was you!"

Jake grinned sheepishly. "Okay, you caught me. I couldn't help it—they smelled so good."

"But what about the peanut butter smell?" Ben asked, crossing his arms.

Jake held up a jar from his pocket. "I added peanut butter to one of the cookies. It's my favorite."

Emma shook her head. "Jake, those cookies were for Santa!"

"I'm sorry," Jake said, his face turning red. "I didn't think it would be a big deal. I didn't know you'd notice."

"Of course we noticed!" Emma said, her voice firm. "Santa always eats the cookies and drinks the milk. Now what are we supposed to leave for him?"

Making Things Right

Jake looked genuinely sorry. "I'll help you bake a new batch," he offered. "I can even clean up afterward."

Emma raised an eyebrow. "Do you promise not to eat any this time?"

"I promise," Jake said.

The three of them spent the next hour baking a fresh batch of cookies. This time, Emma kept a close eye on Jake to make sure no more cookies went missing. By the time they were done, the house once again smelled like Christmas, and the plate was piled high with warm, chocolate chip cookies.

A Christmas Morning Surprise

The next morning, Emma and Ben raced to the living room. The plate of cookies was empty, and the glass of milk was gone.

"He came!" Ben shouted, his face lighting up.

Emma noticed something else: a note written in curly, red handwriting.

Dear Emma and Ben,

Thank you for the delicious cookies! They were the perfect treat after a long night of deliveries. I hear you solved a cookie mystery this year—well done, detectives! Merry Christmas!

Love, Santa

Emma and Ben beamed with pride. Their case was closed, and Christmas was saved.

And as they opened their presents, they couldn't help but laugh when they found one last gift from Santa: a tiny detective kit, complete with a magnifying glass and a notebook.

The End

Chapter 18: The Elf Who Couldn't Wrap

In the bustling workshop of the North Pole, every elf had a role to play. Some elves built toys, some painted intricate designs, and others assembled gadgets. But the most prestigious job of all was gift wrapping—turning every toy into a beautifully wrapped present ready for Christmas morning.

Pip, the smallest elf in the workshop, was desperate to be a gift wrapper. The sight of perfectly folded paper, glossy bows, and sparkling ribbons filled him with joy. But Pip had a problem: no matter how hard he tried, he couldn't wrap a present to save his life.

One day, as Pip stood at the gift-wrapping station, he watched the other elves work with awe. Holly, the lead gift wrapper, folded paper so fast it looked like magic. Ribbon flowed through her hands like silk, forming perfect curls with a single flick of her wrist.

"Come on, Pip!" Holly called with a cheerful grin. "Let's see you wrap that teddy bear."

Pip gulped and picked up the fluffy bear. He placed it on the wrapping paper and pulled the edges together, but the paper crinkled and tore. The tape stuck to his fingers instead of the gift, and when he tried to tie a bow, the ribbon knotted into a mess.

Holly stifled a giggle. "That's... um... creative," she said gently.

"It's terrible," Pip muttered, his cheeks burning with embarrassment.

Over the next few days, Pip practiced nonstop. He stayed in the workshop late into the night, trying to perfect his wrapping skills. But no matter how hard he worked, his gifts came out lumpy, uneven, or wrapped so tightly that the toys nearly broke.

"I'll never be good at this," Pip sighed, slumping onto a stool.

"Don't give up," said Jingle, one of Pip's friends. "You just need more practice."

"I've practiced more than anyone," Pip grumbled. "I'm just not cut out for wrapping."

"Maybe you're thinking too much," Jingle said. "Why don't you try having fun with it?"

"Fun?" Pip repeated, frowning. "How can I have fun when I keep messing up?"

"Wrapping gifts is supposed to bring joy," Jingle said with a wink. "Think about the kids who'll open them on Christmas morning."

The next day, Pip returned to the wrapping station with a new mindset. Instead of worrying about making every fold perfect, he focused on the joy of creating something special. He added extra stickers to one gift, used a bright yellow ribbon on another, and even drew little snowflakes on a piece of plain brown paper.

When Holly came over to inspect his work, she tilted her head. "Well, it's not exactly traditional," she said slowly, "but it's... unique."

"Do you think it's good enough?" Pip asked nervously.

Holly smiled. "It's more than good enough. It's full of personality—and that's what matters."

As Christmas Eve approached, Pip's confidence grew. He found creative ways to wrap even the oddest-shaped toys, like model airplanes and stuffed octopuses. The other elves started asking him for tips on making their gifts more fun and colorful.

On Christmas Eve, Santa stopped by the workshop to check on the preparations. His eyes twinkled as he examined Pip's wrapping.

"Well done, Pip!" Santa said. "These gifts are brimming with Christmas spirit."

"Really?" Pip asked, his eyes wide.

"Absolutely," Santa said with a chuckle. "Sometimes, a little creativity is better than perfection. These gifts will bring so much joy to the children who open them."

Pip beamed with pride. For the first time, he felt like he truly belonged at the wrapping station.

That night, as Santa's sleigh soared into the sky, Pip stood with the other elves, watching the glowing presents disappear into the night. He couldn't wait to imagine the smiles on the children's faces when they saw his colorful, joyful creations.

And as the first snowflakes of Christmas morning fell, Pip realized that wrapping gifts wasn't about being perfect—it was about sharing happiness and love.

The End

Chapter 19: The Reindeer Who Forgot How to Fly

It was just a few days before Christmas, and the North Pole was buzzing with excitement. The elves were finishing the last toys, Santa was double-checking his list, and the reindeer were doing their final practice flights before the big night.

In the training yard, Rudolph was soaring through the sky, his red nose glowing brightly as he led the younger reindeer through loops and dives.

"Great job, everyone!" Rudolph called, landing gracefully in the snow. "You're all ready for Christmas Eve."

But as the other reindeer cheered and celebrated, Rudolph noticed someone sitting off to the side. A young reindeer named Comet Jr. was lying in the snow, his antlers drooping and his wings folded tightly against his sides.

Rudolph trotted over. "Hey, Comet Jr., what's wrong? Aren't you going to join the next flight?"

Comet Jr. sighed. "I can't. I... I forgot how to fly."

Rudolph blinked in surprise. "Forgot how to fly? But you were one of the best last year!"

"I know," Comet Jr. said, his voice trembling. "But I've been too nervous to practice, and now whenever I try, I just fall. I'm afraid I'll mess up in front of everyone."

Rudolph's heart went out to him. He remembered how hard it had been to join the sleigh team when everyone doubted him because of his glowing nose. "Don't worry," Rudolph said gently. "I'll help you get your confidence back."

Step One: Starting Small

The next morning, Rudolph met Comet Jr. in the quiet meadow behind the reindeer barn. "We'll start small," Rudolph said. "No big tricks, no sleigh pulls—just a little jump and glide."

Comet Jr. pawed nervously at the snow. "What if I fall?"

"Then you fall," Rudolph said with a shrug. "And you get back up. Flying takes practice, and everyone stumbles at first."

Comet Jr. took a deep breath and crouched low. He leapt into the air, his wings flapping furiously—but he only managed to hover a few feet before crashing back into the snow.

"Well," Comet Jr. said, spitting out a mouthful of snow, "that went about as badly as I expected."

Rudolph laughed. "It wasn't bad at all! You got off the ground, and that's the hardest part. Let's try again."

Step Two: Building Confidence

Over the next few days, Rudolph worked with Comet Jr. tirelessly. They practiced short flights, worked on balance, and even played games to make flying more fun. Rudolph encouraged him every step of the way, cheering for every small success.

One afternoon, as they practiced gliding, Comet Jr. managed to stay in the air longer than ever before. "I'm doing it!" he shouted, his wings outstretched. "I'm really flying!"

"Great job, Comet Jr.!" Rudolph called, his nose glowing brightly. "You're getting better every day."

Comet Jr. landed with a grin, his confidence starting to grow. But then he frowned. "What if I mess up during the real flight? What if I let Santa down?"

Rudolph placed a hoof on Comet Jr.'s shoulder. "Everyone makes mistakes, even Santa. What matters is that you try your best. And remember, you've got a whole team to support you."

Comet Jr. nodded, his resolve strengthening. "Okay. I'll keep practicing."

Step Three: Facing Fear

On Christmas Eve morning, the final sleigh test arrived. The entire team gathered in the yard, ready to pull Santa's sleigh for the practice run. Comet Jr. stood at the end of the line, his legs trembling.

"You'll be great," Rudolph whispered. "Just remember everything we practiced."

When Santa gave the signal, the reindeer charged forward, their hooves pounding against the snow as they took off. Comet Jr. flapped his wings as hard as he could, and for a moment, he soared with the team. The wind rushed past his face, and his heart swelled with joy.

But then a strong gust of wind hit him, throwing him off balance. Comet Jr. panicked, his wings folding instinctively. He began to fall.

"I can't do it!" he shouted.

"Yes, you can!" Rudolph called, diving toward him. "Open your wings! Trust yourself!"

Comet Jr. took a deep breath and spread his wings wide. The wind caught them, and he steadied himself. With a burst of determination, he flapped hard and rejoined the team.

"I'm flying!" Comet Jr. shouted, his voice full of amazement.

"You're not just flying," Rudolph said with a grin. "You're leading the way!"

Christmas Eve: The Big Moment

That night, as Santa prepared to take off for his worldwide journey, he called the reindeer team together. "Tonight's an important night," Santa said, his voice booming. "We're bringing joy to children everywhere. And I know every one of you is ready."

Comet Jr. stood tall, his wings strong and his confidence shining. When the signal came, he leapt into the air with the rest of the team, pulling the sleigh into the starry sky.

Throughout the flight, Comet Jr. flew flawlessly. He helped navigate through tricky storms, supported another reindeer when they wobbled, and even caught a falling present mid-air.

When the flight was over and they returned to the North Pole, Santa patted Comet Jr. on the back. "Well done, my boy. You've proven yourself tonight."

Comet Jr. beamed with pride. "Thank you, Santa. But I couldn't have done it without Rudolph."

Rudolph smiled, his nose glowing brightly. "You had it in you all along, Comet Jr. You just needed a little push."

That Christmas, Comet Jr. discovered that courage wasn't about never being afraid—it was about trying anyway. And with Rudolph's help, he learned that sometimes, all it takes is a little faith to remember how to fly.

The End

Chapter 20: Santa's New Job

It all started one quiet afternoon in early January, just after Santa's big Christmas Eve journey. The workshop was peaceful for once—no bustling elves, no reindeer training, and no urgent toy orders. Santa sat by the fireplace in his North Pole home, stroking his long white beard and sipping hot cocoa. But despite the cozy atmosphere, he felt a strange emptiness.

Mrs. Claus noticed his furrowed brow. "What's troubling you, dear?" she asked, setting a plate of freshly baked cookies on the table.

Santa sighed deeply. "I'm not sure anyone needs me anymore, Mary. The elves are so efficient, the world has online shopping, and even kids seem to know more about where presents come from than they used to. Maybe it's time for me to... try something new."

Mrs. Claus chuckled. "Santa, you've been bringing joy to children for centuries. You're irreplaceable!"

"But what if I could bring joy in a different way?" Santa said, his eyes twinkling with a spark of an idea. "Maybe it's time I found a new job."

Mrs. Claus raised an eyebrow. "A new job? Well, if that's what you feel you need, you should give it a try."

Job 1: Toy Store Clerk

Santa's first idea was to work in a toy store. After all, who knew toys better than him? He found a small shop in a bustling city and introduced himself to the owner, Mr. Abernathy.

"I'd love to work here," Santa said, shaking Mr. Abernathy's hand. "I have plenty of experience with toys."

"Well, we can always use an extra hand," Mr. Abernathy said, eyeing Santa's red coat and cheerful demeanour. "You can start today."

At first, Santa loved the job. He helped children find the perfect toys, gave advice to parents, and even fixed a few broken trains on the spot. But things took a turn when Santa decided to give away some of the toys for free.

"Christmas spirit should last all year!" Santa said with a grin as he handed a doll to a wide-eyed little girl.

Mr. Abernathy wasn't as enthusiastic. "Santa, we can't just give everything away. We're running a business here!"

"Oh, right," Santa said sheepishly. "I suppose I'm better at giving than selling."

Job 2: Chef

Next, Santa decided to try his hand as a chef. After all, he loved cookies, and Mrs. Claus always said he made the fluffiest pancakes in the North Pole. He joined a local diner, donning an apron over his red suit.

At first, things went well. Customers loved his jolly laugh and generous portions. But Santa's sweet tooth got the better of him. He added so much frosting to the cakes and sugar to the pies that even the sweetest-toothed customers couldn't finish their desserts.

"This is... delightful," one patron said, trying to be polite, "but I don't think I'll need dessert for a week."

The diner's manager gently suggested that Santa might be better suited to eating sweets than making them.

Job 3: Teacher

Santa's next stop was a local school. He loved storytelling, so he applied to be a teacher. The principal, enchanted by Santa's charisma, agreed to let him try teaching a holiday history class.

The children adored Santa's animated storytelling. He told them about the origins of Christmas traditions, reindeer adventures, and even how he started delivering presents. But when Santa accidentally revealed too much about the North Pole's inner workings—like how the elves used "peppermint power" to fuel the sleigh—things got complicated.

"Wait," one child said, her hand shooting up. "Are you the Santa Claus?"

Santa chuckled nervously. "Well, I, uh..."

The principal had to step in, thanking Santa for his time but reminding him that keeping some things a mystery was part of the magic.

Job 4: Pet Groomer

Santa loved animals, so he thought he'd try his hand at being a pet groomer. After all, if he could care for a team of flying reindeer, how hard could it be to groom a few puppies?

It turned out to be harder than he expected. Dogs wriggled, cats scratched, and Santa found himself covered in fur and soap bubbles. One particularly feisty golden retriever knocked over a bucket of water, sending Santa sliding across the floor.

"I think I'll stick to reindeer," Santa muttered, dripping wet as the owner of the golden retriever handed him a towel.

Finding His True Calling

After weeks of trying different jobs, Santa returned to the North Pole feeling defeated. He sat in his favorite chair by the fireplace, staring into the flames.

"I don't think I'm cut out for anything else," Santa said to Mrs. Claus. "Maybe the world doesn't need me anymore."

Mrs. Claus placed a hand on his shoulder. "Oh, Nicholas, the world will always need you. It's not just about the toys. You bring joy, hope, and wonder to people's lives. That's something no one else can do."

Santa thought about her words. He remembered the children's laughter at the toy store, the joy on the customers' faces at the diner, and the excitement of the students in his class. Even when things didn't go perfectly, he had made people smile.

"You're right, Mary," Santa said, his eyes lighting up. "Maybe I don't need a new job. I just need to keep doing what I do best—spreading joy."

Back to the Workshop

With renewed purpose, Santa threw himself back into his work at the North Pole. He visited the elves in the workshop, checked on the reindeer, and started planning for the next Christmas.

On Christmas Eve, as he soared through the sky in his sleigh, Santa felt more grateful than ever. He realized that his role wasn't just about delivering presents—it was about bringing magic and happiness to the world, a job no one else could do.

And as he flew over the twinkling lights of a sleeping town, he laughed his jolly laugh, knowing he was exactly where he was meant to be.

"Ho, ho, ho! Merry Christmas to all, and to all a good night!"

The End

Chapter 21: The Rabbit's Winter Feast

Winter had settled over the forest, covering the ground in a thick blanket of snow. The trees sparkled with frost, and icicles hung like delicate ornaments from the branches. Deep in the heart of the woods, beneath the shelter of a hollowed-out oak tree, a little rabbit named Willow was busily hopping about, gathering scraps of food.

Willow loved winter, but this year had been especially harsh. The snow had come early, and food was scarce. She had managed to collect a few berries and nuts, but it wasn't much.

"I wanted to host a feast for all my friends," Willow said aloud, looking sadly at her small pile of food. "But this is hardly enough for one rabbit, let alone the whole forest."

As she sat thinking, a soft knock came from the edge of her burrow. Willow peeked outside to see her friend Pip, a cheerful squirrel, carrying a bundle of acorns in his tiny paws.

"Hi, Willow!" Pip said brightly. "I heard you were planning a feast. I thought you might need some help."

Willow's ears perked up. "Oh, Pip! That's so kind of you. But I don't have much to offer."

"Nonsense," Pip said, dropping his acorns onto the pile. "Feasts are better when everyone pitches in. Let's see who else can help!"

Word quickly spread through the forest, and soon Willow's burrow was bustling with visitors. Maggie the mole arrived with a basket of mushrooms she had dug up from under the snow. Theo the fox brought a small stash of frozen berries he had hidden in the fall. Even Ollie the owl fluttered in with a few pinecones filled with seeds.

"We'll have a feast yet!" Pip said, clapping his tiny paws.

The animals worked together, sorting the food and deciding how to prepare it. Willow hopped around excitedly, directing her friends. "Maggie, can you clean the mushrooms? Pip, help Theo crush those berries for sauce. Ollie, can you gather some firewood for warmth?"

"On it!" Ollie hooted, flying off toward the edge of the clearing.

As the animals worked, the little pile of food began to grow into a proper feast. There were sweet berry sauces, roasted nuts, mushroom stew, and even a few freshly dug carrots that a family of badgers had brought over.

With the food nearly ready, the animals turned their attention to decorating the clearing for the feast. Willow hopped to a nearby tree and tied strands of ivy around its trunk, while Pip collected pinecones and strung them together with bits of twine.

Maggie and Theo worked together to carve ice lanterns from frozen puddles, placing candles inside to make them glow. As the lanterns lit up the clearing, the snow sparkled like diamonds.

"This is the most beautiful feast I've ever seen," Willow said, her nose twitching with excitement.

"It's not just the feast," Pip said, looking around at their friends. "It's all of us working together."

As the sun set and the forest grew dark, the animals gathered around the feast. Willow hopped up onto a small log to speak.

"Thank you, everyone, for coming together to make this happen," she said, her voice trembling with emotion. "When I thought of hosting a feast, I never imagined it would turn into something so special. You've all shown me what the true spirit of the season is—sharing what we have and helping each other."

The animals cheered, their voices echoing through the snowy woods.

With laughter and chatter, they began the feast. The berry sauce was sweet and tangy, the mushrooms were earthy and warm, and the roasted nuts had just the right crunch. Everyone agreed it was the best meal they'd had all winter.

As the feast wound down and the animals sat contentedly in the glow of the ice lanterns, a gentle snow began to fall. The flakes sparkled as they drifted down, coating the clearing in a fresh, glittering layer of white.

"It's like a gift from the sky," Maggie said, looking up in wonder.

Willow smiled, her heart full. "A perfect ending to a perfect feast."

From that night on, the animals of the forest made the Winter Feast an annual tradition. And every year, they remembered how one little rabbit's dream of sharing brought the whole forest together.

The End

Chapter 22: The Owl and the Snowflake

On a frosty December night, under a sky full of twinkling stars, Ollie the owl perched in his favorite tree at the edge of the forest. The snow-covered world stretched out below him, peaceful and silent. Ollie was a wise and patient owl, known for his calm demeanour and thoughtful ways. But as he gazed at the snowy expanse, he couldn't shake the feeling that he was missing something.

"Christmas," he murmured to himself, "seems to be a time of great excitement for everyone else. But I don't see what's so special about it. It's just another cold winter's day."

Just as Ollie was about to close his eyes for a nap, something fluttered down from the sky and landed on his wing. It was a snowflake—tiny, delicate, and shimmering like a diamond.

"What an intricate little thing," Ollie said, turning his head to study it more closely. But as he stared, the snowflake began to glow faintly. Before Ollie could react, a soft voice spoke.

"Hello, Ollie."

Ollie blinked. "Who said that?"

"I did," the snowflake replied. Its glow brightened, and tiny, sparkling arms stretched outward as if it were alive.

Ollie tilted his head. "A talking snowflake? I must be dreaming."

"You're not dreaming," the snowflake said with a gentle laugh. "I've come to show you the magic of Christmas."

Before Ollie could ask what the snowflake meant, the world around him began to change. The tree branches, once bare and covered in frost, blossomed with twinkling lights. The forest floor sparkled as if dusted with glitter, and a warm, golden glow filled the air.

"What's happening?" Ollie asked, his eyes wide.

"I'm taking you on a journey," the snowflake said. "Christmas isn't just about decorations and presents. It's about the magic that lives in simple, heartfelt moments. Look around."

Ollie flapped his wings and soared higher, taking in the transformed forest. Below, he saw a family of rabbits snuggled together in a hollow log, sharing a meal of foraged berries and nuts. Despite the cold, their faces glowed with happiness.

"Do you see?" the snowflake asked. "Christmas is about togetherness."

Ollie nodded slowly, his feathers ruffling in the cool breeze. "I never thought of it that way."

The snowflake guided Ollie farther into the forest, where he spotted Theo the fox sitting alone by a frozen stream. Theo's tail was wrapped around his body, and his ears drooped.

"Why is Theo so sad?" Ollie asked.

"Theo couldn't find enough food to store for winter," the snowflake explained. "But watch."

As they hovered nearby, Pip the squirrel appeared, carrying a small bundle of nuts and berries. "Theo!" Pip called. "I thought you might need these."

Theo's face lit up with surprise and gratitude. "Thank you, Pip," he said. "I don't know how to repay you."

"You don't have to," Pip replied with a grin. "That's what friends are for."

The snowflake twinkled. "Christmas is also about kindness and generosity, Ollie. Even the smallest gestures can mean the world to someone."

Ollie's heart warmed as he watched Theo and Pip share a laugh. "I've always thought of kindness as something ordinary," Ollie said. "But now it seems... magical."

The snowflake led Ollie to the edge of Pinewood Town, where the townsfolk had gathered in the square. A large Christmas tree stood in the center, its branches adorned with glowing lights and colorful ornaments. Children laughed as they skated on a frozen pond, their scarves trailing behind them like ribbons.

As Ollie perched on a nearby lamppost, he noticed a man handing out cups of hot cocoa. Another group of people was singing carols, their voices harmonizing beautifully in the crisp night air.

"This," the snowflake said softly, "is the joy of Christmas. It's a time when people come together to celebrate love, happiness, and hope."

Ollie watched the scene unfold, his heart filling with a sense of wonder he had never felt before. "I think I understand now," he said. "Christmas isn't just about big, grand gestures. It's about finding beauty in small moments and sharing joy with others."

The snowflake's glow began to dim, and Ollie felt a pang of sadness. "Are you leaving?" he asked.

"My time here is short," the snowflake replied. "But before I go, remember this: Christmas magic isn't something you have to find. It's something you can create, simply by spreading love and kindness wherever you go."

Ollie nodded, his heart brimming with gratitude. "Thank you for showing me, little snowflake."

The snowflake sparkled one last time before it melted away, leaving behind a soft glow that lingered in the air.

That night, Ollie returned to the forest, eager to share what he had learned. He gathered his friends—Pip, Theo, Willow the rabbit, and even Maggie the mole—and invited them to a clearing where he had decorated a small tree with twigs, berries, and pieces of colorful cloth.

"This is for all of you," Ollie said. "A celebration of the magic we create together."

The animals cheered, their laughter echoing through the snowy woods. As they shared stories and treats under the twinkling sky, Ollie felt a warmth in his heart that no winter chill could touch.

And from that night on, Ollie carried the magic of Christmas with him, knowing that even the smallest acts of kindness could light up the world.

The End

Chapter 23: A Penguin's Christmas Journey

The icy wind swept across the vast Antarctic landscape, sending snow swirling in little spirals. Percy the penguin waddled determinedly across the frozen expanse, clutching a small, carefully wrapped package in his flippers. It was Christmas Eve, and Percy had one mission: to deliver his special gift.

The journey had begun earlier that morning when Percy decided that his best friend, Penny, deserved something extraordinary for Christmas. Penny had always been there for Percy—sharing her fish, cheering him on during their swim races, and even keeping him company during the long, cold winters. This year, Percy wanted to give her something as special as her friendship: a rare, golden feather he had found near the cliffs. The feather sparkled like sunlight on ice, and Percy had wrapped it in the softest seaweed he could find, tying it with a strand of kelp.

But Penny's colony was far away, on the other side of the glacier. Percy knew the journey would be difficult, but he was determined to make it. He tucked the package tightly against his chest and set off.

The first part of the journey was smooth. Percy slid on his belly across the ice, the cold wind whipping past him. He loved the rush of speed and the crisp crunch of snow beneath him. The landscape sparkled under the pale sunlight, and for a moment, Percy felt like nothing could go wrong.

But as the day wore on, the weather began to change. Dark clouds rolled in, and the wind grew stronger, biting at Percy's feathers. He tried to push forward, but the snow was blinding, and soon he could barely see a few feet ahead. Percy stopped and huddled behind a jagged piece of ice, trying to catch his breath.

"I can't give up," Percy whispered to himself, clutching the package. "Penny is counting on me."

Just as he was about to set out again, Percy heard a faint sound—a high-pitched whistle carried on the wind. He looked around, squinting through the snow, and spotted a small figure struggling in the storm. It was a young seal pup, tangled in a patch of kelp and unable to move.

Percy waddled over as quickly as he could. "Are you okay?" he called out.

The seal pup shook his head, his eyes wide with fear. "I got caught in this kelp, and I can't get free!"

Without hesitation, Percy used his beak to carefully untangle the kelp, freeing the pup's flippers. "There you go," Percy said. "Are you hurt?"

The pup wiggled his flippers and smiled. "I'm fine now. Thank you! Where are you going in this storm?"

"I'm delivering a Christmas gift to my friend," Percy explained. "Her colony is on the other side of the glacier."

"That's a long way," the pup said, tilting his head. "You're very brave."

Percy smiled. "Friends are worth it."

The pup nodded. "Be careful. And thank you again!"

As the pup disappeared into the storm, Percy felt a little stronger. Helping someone else had warmed him from the inside, giving him the courage to keep going. He pressed forward, pushing through the snow with renewed determination.

The storm began to ease as Percy neared the glacier. The ice was smooth and glassy, stretching out like an endless frozen sea. Percy took a deep breath and stepped onto the glacier, the package still clutched tightly in his flippers. Each step was slow and careful; the ice was slippery, and one wrong move could send him sliding into danger.

Halfway across the glacier, Percy heard a loud crack. He froze, his heart pounding. The ice beneath him was splitting. He scrambled forward as fast as he could, slipping and sliding as the crack grew wider. Just as the ice gave way, Percy leapt to safety, landing hard on solid ground.

He lay there for a moment, panting, then checked the package. It was still safe. "Almost there," Percy said to himself, getting back to his feet.

The final stretch of the journey was uphill, leading to the cliffs where Penny's colony nested. Percy's legs ached, and his feathers were stiff with ice, but he didn't stop. With every step, he thought of Penny's smile and the joy the golden feather would bring her.

At last, Percy reached the top of the cliffs. The view was breathtaking—waves crashing against the icy shore below, the sky painted with shades of pink and orange as the sun dipped toward the horizon. And there, nestled among the rocks, was Penny's colony.

"Percy!" Penny called, waddling over as soon as she spotted him. Her eyes widened when she saw the package in his flippers. "What are you doing here?"

"Merry Christmas, Penny," Percy said, holding out the gift. "This is for you."

Penny unwrapped the package carefully, her beak trembling with excitement. When she saw the golden feather, her eyes filled with wonder.

"Percy, it's beautiful," she said softly. "Where did you find this?"

"Near the cliffs by my colony," Percy said. "It reminded me of you—bright and one of a kind."

Penny smiled, tears glistening in her eyes. "Thank you, Percy. This is the best Christmas gift I've ever received."

As the sun set and the stars began to appear, the two friends sat side by side, watching the waves. Percy's journey had been long and difficult, but seeing Penny's happiness made it all worth it. He realized that Christmas wasn't just about the gifts—it was about the love and effort behind them.

And as the first snowflakes of Christmas morning began to fall, Percy felt a warmth in his heart that no winter chill could touch.

The End

Chapter 24: The Fox's Christmas Gift

Theo the fox padded silently through the snowy forest, his sharp ears twitching at every sound. The snow had fallen heavily that evening, covering the ground in a soft, glistening blanket. The air was cold and crisp, and the moon hung high, casting a silvery glow over the trees. But Theo barely noticed the beauty around him.

His stomach growled, a harsh reminder of the days he'd spent searching for food. Winter was always tough, but this year had been especially hard. The forest seemed quieter, the usual abundance of small creatures and berries nowhere to be found. Hunger gnawed at Theo's belly, and a small voice in his head whispered that he should have left the forest to find food in the nearby village.

But Theo wasn't ready to give up. "There has to be something out here," he muttered to himself, sniffing the air for any sign of a meal.

As he wandered deeper into the forest, Theo came across a small clearing where a pine tree stood alone, its branches heavy with snow. Beneath the tree, something glittered faintly in the moonlight. Curious, Theo crept closer and found a small bundle wrapped in colorful cloth, tied with a simple piece of twine.

Theo's nose twitched. He could smell something delicious—a faint, sugary scent that made his mouth water. Carefully, he nudged the bundle open with his paw and found a handful of sweet-smelling biscuits inside, each shaped like a star. Beside them was a tiny note written in careful, blocky letters.

For anyone in need. Merry Christmas.

Theo blinked at the note, his ears flicking back. He looked around the clearing, but there was no sign of who had left the bundle. The biscuits smelled wonderful, and Theo's first instinct was to eat them all. But as he picked one up with his paw, he hesitated.

He thought of the rabbits huddled in their burrows, the birds fluffing their feathers against the cold, and even the badger family he'd seen trudging through the snow earlier that day. Everyone in the forest was struggling. Everyone was hungry.

Theo sighed and sat back on his haunches, the biscuit still in his paw. "I could eat these all myself," he murmured. "But... maybe someone else needs them more."

The thought tugged at him, stirring something warm and unfamiliar in his chest. Slowly, Theo wrapped the bundle back up and picked it up in his jaws. He turned and began to trot through the forest, his sharp eyes scanning for signs of his neighbours.

The first stop was a hollow log where Theo knew a family of mice lived. He crouched down and placed the bundle at the entrance, gently unwrapping it to reveal the biscuits.

The smallest mouse peeked out, his whiskers quivering. "Theo?" he squeaked nervously. "What are you doing here?"

"Don't worry," Theo said, stepping back. "I'm not here to hunt. I found these biscuits, and I thought you might need them."

The mouse's eyes widened in surprise. Slowly, his family emerged, their tiny noses twitching as they sniffed the air.

"Thank you," the mouse said, his voice trembling. "We haven't had anything to eat for days."

Theo nodded and padded away before they could say more. As he moved through the forest, he felt a strange warmth spreading through him, even though the night was bitterly cold.

His next stop was a small den where a pair of young foxes lived with their mother. Theo placed another biscuit at the entrance and called softly, "There's food here for you."

The mother fox peeked out, her tired eyes lighting up when she saw the biscuit. "Theo, this is so kind of you. Thank you."

Theo dipped his head and continued on, leaving biscuits wherever he thought they were needed most. By the time he returned to the pine tree, there was only one biscuit left in the bundle. He placed it on the ground and sat beside it, his stomach still growling but his heart full.

As he sat there, staring up at the glittering stars, he heard a soft rustle behind him. Turning, he saw a snowy owl perched on a low branch, watching him with curious eyes.

"Why didn't you eat the biscuits yourself?" the owl asked, tilting her head.

Theo shrugged. "I guess I realized I wasn't the only one who was hungry. Sharing them felt... right."

The owl nodded, her feathers shimmering in the moonlight. "That's the spirit of Christmas, Theo. Giving to others, even when it's not easy, is what makes the season special."

Theo smiled, the warmth in his chest glowing even brighter. He looked down at the last biscuit and decided to leave it under the tree, in case someone else needed it.

As the owl flew off into the night, Theo lay down beneath the pine tree, the snow soft beneath him. For the first time in days, he didn't feel empty. The joy of giving had filled him in a way food never could.

And as he drifted off to sleep, the forest around him seemed a little brighter, as if the stars themselves were shining just for him.

The End

Chapter 25: The Bethlehem Star

The night was still and clear, the sky a canvas of deep blue speckled with countless stars. David, a young shepherd, sat on a rocky hillside, keeping watch over his flock. The sheep rested quietly, their soft bleats occasionally breaking the silence. David's older brothers had gone to the nearby village for supplies, leaving him in charge for the night.

It was a night like any other—or so David thought.

He leaned back against a tree, his eyes scanning the heavens. The stars had always fascinated him, their beauty comforting him during the long, lonely nights. But tonight, one star stood out from the rest. It was brighter and larger than anything he had ever seen, its golden glow illuminating the darkness.

David frowned, leaning forward for a better look. "What kind of star is that?" he murmured.

As he stared, the star seemed to pulse with light, as though calling to him. A strange feeling stirred in David's heart—a pull, a whisper urging him to follow.

"Follow the star?" he said aloud, shaking his head. "I can't leave the sheep."

But the feeling didn't fade. If anything, it grew stronger, filling him with a sense of wonder and urgency. David glanced at the flock. They were safe, tucked into a small pen beneath the hill. His brothers would return soon. Surely it would be all right to leave for just a little while.

Making up his mind, David grabbed his staff and began walking, his eyes fixed on the glowing star.

The journey was quiet but filled with a strange energy. The star guided him across fields and rocky paths, its light never wavering. David's sandals crunched against the frosty ground as he pressed on, the cool night air nipping at his face. He wasn't sure where he was going, but he trusted the star to lead the way.

After what felt like hours, David reached the outskirts of a small town. Bethlehem, he realized. He had been here before with his brothers to trade wool, but tonight it looked different. The streets were quiet, the houses dark, as though the town itself was holding its breath.

The star shone brighter now, leading David through narrow alleys and quiet courtyards until he came to a simple stable at the edge of town. The building was small and humble, its walls made of rough wood and stone. But from within came a soft golden light, warm and inviting.

David hesitated at the doorway. "Is this where the star has led me?" he wondered.

A gentle voice broke the silence. "Come in."

David turned to see a man standing nearby, his face kind and weathered. "Don't be afraid," the man said. "The star has brought many visitors tonight."

David nodded, stepping inside. The stable was filled with the soft rustling of hay and the quiet murmur of animals. In the center of the room, a young woman sat cradling a baby in her arms. Her face glowed with peace and joy, and the light of the star seemed to rest upon her.

David's breath caught in his throat. "Is this...?"

"Yes," the man said, standing beside the woman. "This is Jesus, the Savior promised to us all."

David's heart swelled with awe. He dropped to his knees, bowing his head. "I am just a shepherd," he whispered. "Why would the star lead me here?"

"Because the Savior has come for everyone," the man replied. "The humble and the great alike. You followed the star, and now you've seen the greatest gift of all."

Tears filled David's eyes as he gazed at the baby, who seemed to look back at him with a wisdom far beyond his years. In that moment, David felt a warmth unlike anything he had ever known—a love that filled every corner of his being.

As he rose to his feet, David realized he wasn't alone. Others had gathered in the stable: travellers, townsfolk, and even shepherds like himself. They had all been drawn by the star, their faces glowing with wonder and reverence.

David stepped back, letting others approach the baby. His heart was full, his soul at peace. The star had guided him to this place, and he knew his life would never be the same.

When he returned to the hillside later that night, the sheep were still resting, the world quiet once more. But David no longer felt alone. The light of the star and the love of what he had witnessed stayed with him, a constant reminder of the miracle he had seen.

And every time he looked at the night sky, he whispered a quiet prayer of gratitude, knowing that the Bethlehem Star had led him to the greatest gift of all.

The End

Chapter 26: The Stable Animals' Christmas

The stable was quiet and still, the golden glow of the star above Bethlehem filtering through the gaps in the wooden walls. Inside, the animals huddled together, their breath rising in soft clouds in the chilly night air. The donkey, the cow, the sheep, and even the tiny mice had all gathered in one corner, their eyes fixed on the manger at the center of the room.

In the manger lay a baby, his face peaceful, wrapped snugly in cloth. Mary and Joseph sat nearby, watching over him with love and awe. The animals had never seen anything like it, and though they couldn't speak with words, their hearts swelled with the feeling that something extraordinary was happening.

The donkey was the first to break the silence, his deep voice rumbling softly. "I knew there was something special about this journey," he said, his eyes warm with pride. "I carried the mother here, you know. All the way from Nazareth. She was so gentle, and even though she was tired, she never complained."

The cow nodded, her big brown eyes thoughtful. "You brought her safely here, my friend. That was no small task. But I think we all have a part to play tonight."

"What about us?" piped up one of the mice, her whiskers twitching as she peered out from a bundle of hay. "We're just little. What could we possibly do?"

"You've made this stable warmer by nesting here," the cow replied with a gentle moo. "Even the smallest creatures can bring comfort."

The sheep, who had been listening quietly, stepped closer to the group. "I heard the shepherds talking about this baby. They said angels appeared to them, singing songs about peace and joy. The shepherds left everything behind to come see him."

"Angels?" the donkey said, his ears flicking with curiosity. "That explains the feeling in the air. It's as if the whole world is holding its breath."

The mice scurried closer, their tiny eyes wide with wonder. "Do you think he'll remember us? We're not important like angels or shepherds."

The cow gave a soft chuckle. "I don't think it matters whether you're big or small, important or ordinary. Look at him." She motioned toward the baby with her nose. "He came into the world in a humble stable, surrounded by creatures like us. That must mean something."

The animals fell silent, gazing at the child in the manger. His presence seemed to fill the stable with a warmth that chased away the chill of the night.

Outside, the distant murmur of voices grew louder as more visitors arrived. The shepherds entered the stable, their faces lit with awe. They knelt before the manger, whispering words of reverence and wonder. The animals stepped back, giving the humans space but staying close enough to feel part of the moment.

The donkey turned to the others. "We may not speak their language, but we can still honour him in our way. Let's keep the stable quiet and peaceful tonight. He's just a baby, after all."

The mice nodded vigorously, scurrying back to their nest. The cow settled down in the hay, her soft breath warming the air. The sheep lay close to the manger, their woolly bodies creating a cozy barrier against the cold. Even the rooster, who usually couldn't resist crowing, tucked his head under his wing and stayed silent.

As the night stretched on, the stable remained a sanctuary of calm and warmth. The animals watched as visitors came and went, each bringing their own gifts and prayers. They didn't have gold, frankincense, or myrrh, but they gave what they could: their presence, their warmth, and their quiet devotion.

When dawn broke over Bethlehem, the star above the stable still shone brightly. The baby stirred in his manger, and the animals felt a deep sense of peace. They had been witnesses to something miraculous, and though they couldn't explain it, they knew their lives—and the world—would never be the same.

Years later, the story of that night would be told and retold, and though the animals' part might be small, it was no less important. For in their quiet way, they had shown that even the humblest creatures can honour the greatest gift of all.

The End

Chapter 27: The Little Drummer Boy's Friend

The desert air was cool as the stars lit the path toward Bethlehem. Among the travellers making their way to the little town was a boy named Ezra, his sandals kicking up dust as he trudged along the rocky road. Slung over his shoulder was a small drum, its leather surface worn but loved. Ezra had played his drum for as long as he could remember, tapping out rhythms that seemed to echo his heart.

Ezra wasn't alone on his journey. Beside him walked Daniel, a younger boy with wide, curious eyes. Daniel was quiet, often looking to Ezra for guidance. The two were close, having grown up in the same village and sharing a bond like brothers.

"I still don't understand," Daniel said, breaking the silence. "Why are we going to Bethlehem?"

"Because something amazing is happening," Ezra replied. "I heard the shepherds say a great King has been born. People from all over are bringing him gifts."

Daniel frowned. "But we don't have anything to give."

Ezra patted his drum. "We have this. Sometimes a song is worth more than gold."

The boys arrived in Bethlehem as the stars glittered brightly overhead. The streets were quiet, most of the town asleep. But as they reached the outskirts, they saw a small crowd gathered around a humble stable. A warm golden light spilled out from the wooden walls, and the air buzzed with a quiet reverence.

Ezra and Daniel hesitated at the edge of the crowd. People were carrying gifts—fine cloth, jars of oil, and even gold coins. The boys exchanged a glance, their simple clothes and empty hands suddenly feeling out of place.

"We can't go in there," Daniel whispered. "We don't belong."

Ezra frowned, clutching his drum. "Why not? The King came for everyone, didn't he?"

Daniel hesitated, but Ezra was already moving toward the stable. The younger boy followed, his heart pounding.

Inside the stable, Ezra and Daniel froze. There, lying in a manger filled with hay, was a baby. His tiny face glowed with peace, his eyes closed as if dreaming. Beside him sat his mother and father, their expressions full of love and awe.

Ezra's breath caught in his throat. The baby didn't look like a king—not the kind he had imagined. There was no crown, no throne, just the quiet simplicity of a child wrapped in cloth. But as Ezra gazed at him, he felt something stir in his heart—a sense of wonder and purpose.

"Play your drum," Daniel whispered, nudging Ezra. "It's all we have."

Ezra hesitated. The room was filled with important-looking people, their fine gifts gleaming in the lantern light. What could a simple song offer compared to gold and jewels?

But then the baby stirred, his tiny hand reaching out. Ezra swallowed his doubt and stepped forward. Slowly, he knelt beside the manger, his drum resting on his lap.

"This is for you," Ezra said softly.

He began to play, tapping out a gentle rhythm that echoed through the stable. The sound was simple yet beautiful, each beat carrying a quiet reverence. As Ezra played, the room seemed to grow warmer, the light brighter. The baby opened his eyes, gazing at Ezra with a look that made the boy's heart swell.

When the song ended, the stable was silent. Then, one by one, the people in the room began to smile. Even the animals seemed calmer, their breaths slow and steady.

"That was wonderful," Daniel whispered. "I think he liked it."

Ezra looked at the baby, who now slept peacefully once more. "It wasn't much," Ezra said, "but it was from the heart."

As the boys left the stable, Ezra handed Daniel his drum. "Here," he said. "It's yours now."

Daniel's eyes widened. "But it's your drum."

Ezra smiled. "I've learned something tonight. Kindness isn't about what you give—it's about how you give it. You can play this drum and share your own songs. That's more important than me keeping it."

Daniel hugged the drum tightly, tears in his eyes. "Thank you, Ezra."

The boys walked back through the quiet streets, the sound of their laughter filling the air. And though they didn't have gold or jewels, they carried with them the most precious gift of all: the joy of giving from the heart.

The End

Chapter 28: The Christmas Candle

The wind howled through the snowy hills, carrying with it the bitter chill of a winter's night. Clara wrapped her shawl tighter around her shoulders, her heart heavy as she trudged forward through the deep snow. Behind her, her young son Samuel and her husband Jacob followed closely, their footsteps weary. They had been traveling for hours, hoping to reach the nearby village before the storm grew worse, but the path had vanished beneath the snow.

"We should stop," Jacob said, his voice strained. "The storm's too strong, and we'll lose our way if we keep going."

"But where will we go?" Clara asked, her breath visible in the frosty air. "There's nothing but trees and snow for miles."

Samuel, clutching Clara's hand, looked up at her with wide, tearful eyes. "Mama, I'm scared."

Clara knelt beside him, brushing the snow from his hat. "Don't worry, sweetheart. We'll find a way."

Just as she spoke, a faint light flickered in the distance. Clara squinted through the swirling snow. "Jacob, look!" she said, pointing toward the glow. "Do you see that?"

Jacob turned, his tired eyes narrowing. "A light... It could be a house."

"Or someone with a fire," Clara said, hope rising in her chest. "We have to follow it."

The family pressed on, their footsteps quickening despite their exhaustion. The light grew brighter with each step, its golden glow cutting through the storm like a beacon. Finally, they reached the source: a single candle sitting in the window of a small stone cottage.

Clara knocked on the door, her hand trembling from the cold. After a moment, it creaked open to reveal an elderly woman with kind eyes and a warm smile.

"Oh my," the woman said, her voice soft and welcoming. "You poor dears—come in, quickly."

The family stepped inside, the warmth of the cottage washing over them like a balm. A fire crackled in the hearth, and the room smelled of freshly baked bread. The woman helped Clara remove Samuel's wet coat and guided them to the fire.

"I'm Edna," the woman said as she handed them blankets. "You're lucky you found your way here. This storm is fierce."

"We saw your candle," Jacob said, his voice filled with gratitude. "It led us here."

Edna smiled. "That's its purpose. Every Christmas Eve, I place a candle in the window for travellers who might need a little light to guide them."

"Thank you," Clara said, her eyes brimming with tears. "You saved us."

As the family warmed themselves by the fire, Edna brought out bowls of stew and thick slices of bread. They ate gratefully, the food filling their empty stomachs and reviving their spirits. Samuel, his cheeks flushed from the warmth, smiled for the first time that night.

"Your candle is magic," he said between bites. "It led us through the storm."

Edna chuckled, her eyes twinkling. "Not magic, dear—just hope. A little light can go a long way when the night is dark."

After dinner, Edna brought out a small box filled with candles. She handed one to Clara, its wax smooth and unblemished. "Take this with you," Edna said. "When you leave tomorrow, light it in your own window. Pass the light on."

Clara held the candle close, her heart swelling with gratitude. "We will," she promised. "Thank you for everything."

The next morning, the storm had passed, leaving the world blanketed in a dazzling layer of snow. The family bid Edna farewell, their hearts full of warmth and hope. With the directions she had given them, they easily found their way to the village.

That evening, in the small inn where they were staying, Clara placed the candle in the window and lit it. Its golden glow illuminated the room, and as the family gathered around it, they felt a sense of peace.

In the years that followed, Clara kept Edna's tradition alive. Every Christmas Eve, she placed a candle in the window, its light a symbol of hope for anyone who might be lost or in need. And though the storms of life came and went, the light of the Christmas candle always shone, reminding them that even in the darkest times, a little light can lead the way.

The End

Chapter 29: The Angel's Gift

In a quiet village nestled at the base of rolling hills, young Anna sat on the church steps, her chin resting in her hands. The stars sparkled brightly overhead, their light reflecting off the fresh snow that blanketed the ground. It was Christmas Eve, and the church was filled with families singing carols and celebrating. But Anna, who had come alone, couldn't bring herself to join in.

Her family had little this year. The harsh winter had left their crops barren, and they had no gifts to exchange or treats to share. Anna felt as if she had nothing to give, not to her family, her friends, or even to Baby Jesus.

As she sighed, a soft sound caught her attention—a faint rustling, like wings brushing the air. She looked up and gasped. Standing before her was a radiant figure, wrapped in shimmering light. The figure had a kind face, and from its back stretched delicate, glowing wings.

"Don't be afraid," the angel said gently, its voice soft as a breeze. "My name is Gabriel. I've come to ask for your help."

Anna blinked in astonishment. "You... need my help?"

Gabriel nodded, his expression serious. "I've been sent to deliver a gift to Jesus, but it's gone missing. It was a simple, beautiful thing—a golden lily crafted by the stars themselves. I believe it was lost somewhere nearby."

Anna stood, her heart racing. "A gift for Jesus? How could I help with something so important?"

"You have a pure heart, Anna," Gabriel said with a warm smile. "That is the greatest help of all."

Without hesitation, Anna agreed to help. Gabriel led her through the snow-covered village and into the surrounding hills. The stars overhead seemed to glow brighter, casting a soft light on their path. Anna searched carefully, her eyes scanning every snowy bush and rocky crevice.

"Do you think it's far?" Anna asked as they climbed higher.

"I don't know," Gabriel admitted. "But I have faith we will find it."

As they reached a small clearing, Anna spotted something glinting in the snow. She hurried forward and knelt down, brushing the snow away. But her excitement faded as she realized it was just a broken shard of ice.

Gabriel knelt beside her. "Don't lose hope," he said gently. "Even when it seems hard, the journey is part of the gift."

Anna nodded, though doubt gnawed at her heart. Still, she pressed on, determined to help the angel.

Hours passed, and the night grew colder. Anna's hands were numb, her breath forming little clouds in the frosty air. But just as she was about to suggest turning back, she saw something unusual—a faint golden glow coming from beneath a nearby tree.

"Over there!" she cried, pointing.

The two of them hurried to the tree. Nestled among its roots was a delicate golden lily, its petals shimmering with a light that seemed to come from within. Anna carefully picked it up, cradling it in her hands as though it might break.

"You found it," Gabriel said, his voice full of awe. "The gift."

Anna looked at the flower, its glow warming her fingers. "It's so beautiful," she whispered. "It's perfect for Jesus."

Gabriel smiled, his wings rustling softly. "You've done something wonderful tonight, Anna. You've shown kindness, perseverance, and faith. Those are gifts as precious as any golden flower."

As they made their way back to the village, Gabriel stopped in front of the church. The light from the windows spilled onto the snow, and the sound of carols drifted through the air.

"This is where we part, Anna," the angel said. "I will deliver the gift from here."

Anna hesitated. "But I didn't really do anything. You could have found it on your own."

Gabriel knelt, looking her in the eyes. "Your willingness to help, even when you felt small or unsure, is the greatest gift of all. Never doubt the value of a kind heart."

Before Anna could respond, Gabriel rose, the golden lily shining in his hands. With a gentle wave, he lifted into the air, his wings glowing like the morning sun. Anna watched as he disappeared into the night sky, her heart full of wonder.

When Anna returned home, the doubts she had carried earlier were gone. She realized that even without material gifts, she had so much to offer—her love, her kindness, and her willingness to help. And that Christmas, as she sat with her family around the fire, she felt richer than ever before.

Far away, in a humble stable in Bethlehem, a golden lily shone brightly beside the manger, its light a testament to a young girl's faith and the angel who had trusted her with an important task.

The End

Chapter 30: The Town's First Christmas Tree

In the little town of Willow Creek, Christmas was a quiet affair. Families celebrated in their own homes, exchanging small gifts and singing carols by the fire. But the town itself was bare—no lights, no decorations, and certainly no Christmas tree in the square. It had always been that way, and most of the townsfolk didn't mind.

Except for a group of children who thought Christmas in Willow Creek could be so much more.

Nine-year-old Clara sat on the steps of the schoolhouse with her friends Peter, Lucy, and James. The air was cold, and the first flakes of snow had begun to fall, but the children didn't notice. They were too busy planning.

"We should have a Christmas tree in the town square," Clara said, her breath fogging in the chilly air. "A big one, with lights and ornaments and everything!"

Peter, who always had big ideas, nodded eagerly. "And we could all decorate it together! Everyone in town could bring something—like ribbons or candles."

"But how would we even get a tree?" Lucy asked, pulling her scarf tighter around her neck. "And do you really think the grown-ups would agree?"

Clara frowned. The adults in Willow Creek weren't unkind, but they were practical. Many thought that things like Christmas trees were frivolous. "We'll convince them," she said firmly. "If we can get everyone to help, they'll see how wonderful it could be."

The next day, the children began their mission. They went door to door, sharing their idea with the townsfolk. At first, many of the adults were sceptical.

"A tree in the square?" said Mrs. Harper, the baker. "Who's going to decorate it?"

"We'll all decorate it together," Clara said. "It'll bring everyone in town closer, like a big family."

"And who's going to pay for the lights and ornaments?" Mr. Grayson, the blacksmith, grumbled.

"Everyone can bring something from home," Peter suggested. "Old ribbons, scraps of fabric, or anything they think would look nice."

Slowly, their enthusiasm began to spread. Mrs. Harper smiled, imagining the tree lit up against the snowy backdrop. "Well," she said, "I do have some extra red ribbon I could bring."

"I have some old lanterns that might work," added Mr. Grayson, his gruff tone softening. "They'd look good on a tree."

By the end of the week, the whole town was buzzing with excitement. The children had convinced nearly everyone to help, and Mr. Grayson volunteered to chop down a tree from the nearby woods. On the morning of Christmas Eve, the townsfolk gathered in the square as Mr. Grayson arrived with the tree tied to his cart. It was tall and full, its branches dusted with fresh snow.

"It's perfect!" Lucy exclaimed, clapping her hands.

Everyone set to work. The children hung ribbons and paper chains they had made in school, while the adults brought whatever they could spare—candles, shiny pots, colorful scraps of fabric, and even a few small bells. Mr. Grayson's lanterns were carefully tied to the branches, and Mrs. Harper hung gingerbread cookies shaped like stars.

By the time the sun set, the tree was a dazzling display of creativity and community. The lanterns glowed warmly, casting light over the ornaments, and the bells jingled softly in the winter breeze.

The townsfolk gathered around the tree, their faces lit with awe. Someone began to sing a carol, and soon everyone joined in, their voices filling the square. For the first time, Willow Creek felt alive with the true spirit of Christmas—joy, togetherness, and love.

As the last notes of the carol faded, Clara looked around at the smiling faces of her neighbours. "I knew we could do it," she said softly.

"And we'll do it every year from now on," Mr. Grayson said, his voice warm. "This is the start of a new tradition."

Clara's heart swelled with pride and happiness. The little group of children had brought the town together, and their first Christmas tree had done more than brighten the square—it had united the people of Willow Creek in a way they'd never imagined.

From that year on, the town's Christmas tree became the centrepiece of every holiday season, a symbol of what could be achieved when everyone came together with open hearts and a shared purpose.

The End

Chapter 31: The Snowstorm Surprise

The town of Silver Hollow was nestled in a quiet valley surrounded by snow-covered mountains. Its streets were always lively during the holidays, with twinkling lights on every house, carolers singing in the square, and a big Christmas market where neighbours gathered to buy gifts, share stories, and sip warm cider. Christmas in Silver Hollow was always magical, and this year promised to be no different.

That is, until the snowstorm came.

It started two days before Christmas, with soft flurries falling from a grey sky. At first, the townsfolk admired the snow, thinking it would add to the festive atmosphere. But by nightfall, the wind had picked up, and the flurries turned into a blizzard. Snow piled high in the streets, cutting off roads and leaving homes buried. By morning, Silver Hollow was completely blanketed, and the once-bustling town square was eerily quiet.

Mayor Andrews called an emergency meeting at the town hall. The streets were impassable, and everyone was struggling just to clear paths from their front doors. Worst of all, the storm had damaged the power lines, leaving the town without electricity.

"We can't have Christmas like this," Mrs. Harper, the owner of the bakery, said, shaking her head. "No lights, no market... It'll be so dreary."

"It's not just about the decorations," said Mr. Walker, the school principal. "People count on this time of year to bring us together. Without it, it'll feel like any other day."

The room fell silent as the townsfolk exchanged worried looks. Then, from the back of the room, a small voice piped up.

"Why can't we make Christmas happen anyway?" It was Lily, a girl no older than eight, bundled up in a bright red scarf. "Christmas isn't about the lights or the market. It's about helping each other, right?"

The mayor smiled, his face softening. "You're absolutely right, Lily. If we all pitch in, we can still make this Christmas special."

The next morning, Silver Hollow came alive with activity. Neighbours bundled up and ventured into the snow, shovelling paths and clearing roads together. Farmers brought sleighs into town to transport firewood, blankets, and food to those who needed it. The blacksmith, Mr. Tully, used his tools to repair broken sleds and make lanterns that could be used for light.

In the square, a group of children worked to build a giant snowman, using carrots and scarves donated by their neighbours. "He can be our Christmas mascot!" one boy said, laughing as he balanced a hat on the snowman's head.

Meanwhile, the town's musicians—armed with flutes, violins, and a battered old accordion—gathered near the snowman, filling the square with cheerful carols. Their music lifted everyone's spirits as they worked.

Inside the bakery, Mrs. Harper and a group of volunteers were busy baking cookies and pies, using wood-fired stoves to replace the electric ovens. The smell of cinnamon and sugar wafted through the air, drawing curious townsfolk to the bakery door.

"Come in!" Mrs. Harper called, handing out warm cookies to anyone who passed. "Take one for yourself and one for a neighbour!"

At the school, Mr. Walker and a team of parents were wrapping homemade gifts. They used whatever materials they could find—scraps of fabric, bits of ribbon, and even old newspapers—to create packages filled with simple treasures: handmade ornaments, jars of jam, and knitted scarves.

"We'll deliver these to every home in town," Mr. Walker said. "No one should feel left out this Christmas."

As the sun set on Christmas Eve, the townsfolk gathered in the square, their faces glowing in the flickering light of lanterns and candles. Snow still covered the rooftops, but the streets were filled with laughter and warmth. The children's snowman stood proudly in the center of the square, surrounded by a circle of candles that cast a golden glow.

Mayor Andrews stepped forward, his voice carrying over the crowd. "Tonight, we've shown what Christmas truly means. It's not about decorations or gifts—it's about coming together as a community. This year, despite the storm, we've made Silver Hollow brighter than ever."

The crowd cheered, their voices rising into the cold night air. Then, with a nod from the mayor, the musicians began to play, and the townsfolk joined hands, singing carols under the stars.

Lily stood with her family, her cheeks red from the cold but her eyes shining with happiness. She looked around at the smiling faces, the glowing lanterns, and the snow-covered streets filled with joy.

"This is the best Christmas ever," she whispered to her mother.

And as the carols echoed through the valley, the people of Silver Hollow knew that, despite the storm, they had created something truly magical—a Christmas filled with love, kindness, and the unbreakable spirit of their community.

The End

Chapter 32: The Bakery's Christmas Miracle

In the heart of the snowy town of Hollybrook, Mrs. Maple's bakery was the warmest, sweetest place to be during the holidays. The scent of freshly baked bread, cinnamon rolls, and sugar cookies filled the air, drawing townsfolk in for a treat or just to chat with Mrs. Maple. She was known not only for her delicious creations but for her generosity—on Christmas Eve, she always gave away treats to anyone who came by, ensuring no one went without a little holiday cheer.

This year, however, things were different. The season had been busier than ever, and by the morning of Christmas Eve, Mrs. Maple realized with a sinking heart that her cupboards were nearly bare. She had just enough flour for one loaf of bread, and her jars of sugar, butter, and spices were scraped clean. Even her shelves of candies and decorations, usually brimming with color, were empty.

"I can't believe it," Mrs. Maple said, sitting down at her kitchen table. "How can I make Christmas special for the town with no ingredients?"

The bell above the bakery door jingled, and Mrs. Maple looked up to see a small boy named Henry peeking inside. His coat was patched, and his cheeks were red from the cold.

"Good morning, Mrs. Maple," Henry said shyly. "Are you still giving away treats today?"

Mrs. Maple's heart ached. Henry's family didn't have much, and she knew how much he looked forward to her Christmas cookies. "I... I'm not sure, Henry," she said honestly. "I've run out of ingredients."

Henry's face fell. "Oh. That's okay. I just came to wish you a Merry Christmas."

As he turned to leave, Mrs. Maple called after him. "Wait, Henry! Maybe you can help me think of something."

Henry's eyes lit up. "What do you mean?"

Together, Mrs. Maple and Henry brainstormed ways to make Christmas magic without the usual ingredients. They searched the cupboards and found a few forgotten items: a handful of raisins, a half-empty jar of honey, and a bag of oats. Mrs. Maple smiled. "It's not much, but maybe it's enough."

Henry helped Mrs. Maple mix the oats, honey, and raisins into small clusters, pressing them into shapes with cookie cutters. They baked them until they were golden and fragrant. The smell filled the bakery, and soon, curious townsfolk began to peek inside.

"Mrs. Maple, what are you making?" asked Mrs. Harper, the florist, as she stepped into the shop.

"Something new," Mrs. Maple said with a smile, holding out one of the oat clusters. "Would you like to try?"

Mrs. Harper took a bite and grinned. "Delicious! Can I take a few for my family?"

"Of course," Mrs. Maple said. "But there's a catch. If you take some, you have to bring something to share—a little sugar, a pinch of spice, or whatever you have at home."

Mrs. Harper nodded eagerly. "I'll be back!"

Word spread quickly, and soon, townsfolk were streaming into the bakery, bringing whatever ingredients they could spare. Bags of flour, jars of jam, sticks of butter, and handfuls of nuts and dried fruit began to fill Mrs. Maple's shelves. With each donation, Mrs. Maple and Henry created new treats: buttery shortbread, spiced fruit bars, and honey-drizzled cakes.

Everyone in town pitched in, from the blacksmith who brought molasses to the schoolteacher who arrived with a basket of fresh eggs. Even the mayor stopped by with a jar of peppermint candies, which Mrs. Maple crushed into festive toppings.

By evening, the bakery was transformed. The counters were piled high with trays of colorful, fragrant treats, and the air buzzed with laughter and excitement. Mrs. Maple and Henry handed out cookies and cakes to every visitor, making sure no one left empty-handed.

As the last rays of sunlight faded and the stars appeared in the sky, Mrs. Maple stepped outside with Henry to admire the glowing windows of the bakery. The entire town square was alive with holiday cheer, thanks to the treats everyone had helped create.

"Mrs. Maple," Henry said, tugging on her sleeve, "we did it. We made Christmas special."

Mrs. Maple knelt down, her eyes shining. "No, Henry. We didn't do it. The whole town did. This wasn't just my miracle—it was ours."

Henry grinned, his hands clutching a small bag of cookies he planned to share with his family. "It's the best Christmas ever."

Mrs. Maple looked out at the happy faces of her neighbours and nodded. "Yes, it truly is."

And from that year on, Hollybrook's Christmas Eve tradition wasn't just about the treats—it was about the magic that happened when a community came together to share and create something special.

The End

Chapter 33: Grandma's Secret Recipe

The kitchen was warm and cozy, a stark contrast to the swirling snow outside. The smell of cinnamon and vanilla hung in the air as Ellie stood on her tiptoes, peering over the counter. Her grandmother, a kind woman with silver hair tied back in a neat bun, was kneading dough with practiced hands.

"Grandma," Ellie said, her voice full of curiosity, "Mom said you used to make a special Christmas treat when she was little. Why don't you make it anymore?"

Grandma paused, her hands resting on the dough. Her eyes grew distant, and a soft smile touched her lips. "Ah, you mean the Christmas Star Pastries," she said. "I haven't made those in years."

"Why not?" Ellie asked.

Grandma wiped her hands on her apron and sat down at the table, motioning for Ellie to join her. "The recipe is very special. It was passed down from my grandmother, and we only made it for Christmas. But over the years, I stopped. It's a bit complicated, and I wasn't sure anyone remembered it."

Ellie's eyes lit up. "I want to remember it! Can we make them together?"

Grandma chuckled. "It's been a long time, Ellie. But if you're willing to help, we can give it a try."

Grandma retrieved an old, weathered cookbook from the shelf. Its pages were yellowed and dotted with stains from years of use. She carefully turned the pages until she found the recipe, handwritten in elegant script: Christmas Star Pastries.

"First, we'll need to gather the ingredients," Grandma said, scanning the list. "Flour, sugar, butter, cinnamon, and a few other things."

Ellie raced around the kitchen, collecting what they needed. "Got the flour!" she said, lugging the heavy bag to the counter. "And the cinnamon!"

Grandma smiled as she set up the mixing bowls. "Good work, Ellie. Now, let's get started."

Ellie watched closely as Grandma measured out the flour, sugar, and spices. "Why is it called the Christmas Star?" Ellie asked, sprinkling cinnamon into the bowl.

"Because the pastries are shaped like stars," Grandma explained. "And when they bake, they puff up, just like a shining star in the sky."

Together, they mixed the dough, adding butter and a splash of vanilla. Ellie giggled as flour dusted her hands and nose. "This is fun!"

"Baking always is," Grandma said, laughing. "Especially when you're making something special."

Next came the tricky part—rolling out the dough and cutting it into star shapes. Grandma showed Ellie how to use a small knife to create the points of the stars, her hands steady and precise.

"You're a natural," Grandma said as Ellie carefully shaped her first pastry.

After the stars were cut, they filled the centres with a mixture of cinnamon sugar and a dollop of Grandma's homemade jam. "The filling is what makes them extra special," Grandma said, her eyes twinkling. "It's like a surprise in every bite."

Once the pastries were assembled, they placed them on a baking sheet and slid them into the oven. Ellie sat by the oven door, her face pressed against the glass. "How long will it take?" she asked impatiently.

"Not long," Grandma said, joining her. "But good things are worth waiting for."

When the timer dinged, Grandma opened the oven, and the smell of warm cinnamon filled the room. The pastries were golden and puffed, their star shapes perfectly formed. Ellie clapped her hands in delight. "They look just like stars!"

Grandma set the tray on the counter to cool. She dusted the pastries with powdered sugar, making them look as though they'd been kissed by snow. "There," she said. "Just like my grandmother used to make."

Ellie couldn't wait to taste one. She took a bite, and her eyes widened. "Grandma, these are amazing!"

Grandma smiled, her heart full. "I'm glad you think so, Ellie. You've brought this recipe back to life. Maybe we can make it a tradition again."

Ellie beamed. "Every Christmas, just like your grandmother did."

That evening, Ellie and Grandma shared the pastries with the rest of the family. As they sat by the fire, laughing and telling stories, Grandma looked at Ellie and thought how wonderful it was to pass on a piece of her past to the next generation.

From that Christmas on, the Christmas Star Pastries became the highlight of every holiday, a symbol of love, tradition, and the magic of baking together.

The End

Chapter 34: A Christmas Carolling Adventure

The snow fell softly on the small town of Evergreen Hollow, blanketing the streets and rooftops in white. It was Christmas Eve, and the air buzzed with excitement as the townsfolk hurried about, finishing their holiday preparations. But for a group of neighbourhood kids, the night promised an adventure.

Lila, the unofficial leader of the group, stood on the steps of her house, holding a handwritten list of carols. "All right," she said, adjusting her scarf. "We'll start on Elm Street and work our way around the square. Are we ready?"

Her friends—Sam, Mia, and Jamie—nodded eagerly. Each carried a lantern, its golden light flickering in the frosty air. They weren't professional singers, but their hearts were full of holiday spirit, and they were determined to spread as much cheer as possible.

"We should practice first," Mia said, tugging her mittens tighter. "What if we forget the words?"

Jamie grinned. "We'll just hum really loud."

Lila laughed. "Let's give it a shot. How about 'Jingle Bells' to start?"

They launched into the song, their voices blending with the crunch of snow underfoot. Despite a few off-key notes, their enthusiasm carried them through, and soon they were laughing and clapping along to their own music.

Their first stop was the Thompsons' house, a cozy brick home with a glowing wreath on the door. Lila knocked, and the group began to sing as soon as the door opened. The Thompsons—an elderly couple with warm smiles—listened with delight, clapping along and offering the kids cookies when they finished.

"Thank you, dears," Mrs. Thompson said, her eyes twinkling. "It's been years since anyone's come carolling. You've made our night."

The kids beamed, their confidence growing as they moved on to the next house. They sang for the Parkers, who joined in on the choruses, and for Mr. Howard, who was so moved he wiped a tear from his eye.

As they approached the town square, their voices carried through the crisp night air, drawing the attention of passersby. Families paused their shopping, children pressed their noses against frosty windows, and shopkeepers stepped outside to listen.

The kids decided to sing "Silent Night" next, but as they began, Sam's voice faltered. "I don't think I can sing this one," he whispered to Lila. "It's too high."

Before Lila could respond, Jamie stepped forward. "I'll take the lead."

Jamie was usually quiet, preferring to stay in the background, but as he sang the opening notes, his voice rang out clear and beautiful. The group stared in amazement—none of them had realized Jamie had such a talent.

By the second verse, they had joined in, their voices rising in harmony. The square fell silent, everyone captivated by the music. Even the snow seemed to pause, as though the world itself were listening.

When the song ended, the square erupted in applause. Jamie's cheeks turned bright red, but he couldn't hide his smile. "I didn't think I could do that," he said, his voice shy.

"You were amazing!" Mia said, clapping him on the back.

Lila grinned. "You've been holding out on us, Jamie."

Encouraged, Jamie took the lead on the next few songs, his confidence growing with every note. The group sang for hours, their voices weaving through the town and filling it with the warmth of Christmas cheer.

As the night wore on, the kids made their final stop at the town's community center, where a group of families had gathered to escape the cold. They sang every song they knew, ending with a rousing rendition of "We Wish You a Merry Christmas." The families clapped and cheered, their faces glowing with gratitude.

"You've brought so much joy tonight," one woman said, holding her young daughter close. "Thank you for reminding us what Christmas is all about."

When the kids finally returned to Lila's house, tired but happy, they gathered in the living room with mugs of hot cocoa. The night had been more magical than any of them had imagined.

"I think we found something special tonight," Lila said, looking at Jamie. "You've got an incredible voice."

Jamie shrugged, but his smile gave him away. "It felt good to sing," he admitted. "Maybe we could do this every year."

"Definitely," Mia said. "And next year, we'll have more songs and more stops!"

The friends laughed, clinking their mugs together in a toast. They hadn't just spread Christmas cheer that night—they had discovered a hidden talent, strengthened their friendship, and created a new tradition for their little town.

And as the snow continued to fall softly outside, the spirit of their carolling adventure lingered in the hearts of everyone they had touched.

The End

Chapter 35: The Alien Who Loved Christmas

The small town of Evergreen Grove sparkled with Christmas cheer. Twinkling lights hung from every rooftop, wreaths adorned every door, and the scent of pine and cinnamon filled the air. On a quiet hill just outside town, an unexpected visitor was taking it all in.

Zorb, a curious alien from the planet Luminara, had landed his spacecraft in the middle of the snowy woods. His mission was simple: to observe Earth's traditions and learn about its culture. As he wandered closer to the edge of town, his glowing blue eyes widened at the sight of the decorations and bustling streets.

"What are all these strange, glowing things?" Zorb muttered to himself. "And why do these Earthlings seem so... happy?"

His translator chip picked up snatches of conversation as humans passed by.

"Merry Christmas!" one child shouted to another.

"Christmas?" Zorb said, tilting his head. "I must find out what this 'Christmas' is."

Zorb's first stop was the town square, where a massive Christmas tree stood surrounded by people singing carols. He crouched behind a snow-covered bush, his shimmering green skin blending with the shadows. The humans were holding small books and singing together, their voices filling the air with warmth.

"What a curious ritual," Zorb whispered. "It appears to involve synchronized vocalizations."

Suddenly, one of the singers, a boy named Max, spotted Zorb's glowing eyes through the bush. "Hey!" Max called, stepping closer. "Who's there?"

Zorb froze, unsure of what to do. But Max was too quick. He pushed aside the branches and gasped. "Whoa! Are you... an alien?"

Zorb stood to his full height, towering over Max but raising his hands in a gesture of peace. "Yes, I am Zorb from the planet Luminara. Please do not be alarmed. I am here to learn."

Max's fear melted into curiosity. "Learn about what?"

"This... 'Christmas,'" Zorb said, gesturing toward the tree and the carolers. "Your traditions are unlike anything I have seen on my home planet."

Max grinned. "Well, you've come to the right place. Christmas is the best! I can show you everything."

Max brought Zorb to his house, where his family was busy decorating their Christmas tree. Max's little sister, Lily, was hanging ornaments while their parents strung lights around the branches.

"Mom! Dad!" Max said as he burst through the door. "This is Zorb. He's an alien, and he wants to learn about Christmas!"

Max's parents exchanged surprised glances but welcomed Zorb with open arms. "Well," Max's mom said, "you've come on the perfect night. We're just about to finish decorating the tree."

Zorb watched as Lily carefully placed a shiny red ornament on a branch. "What is the purpose of this activity?" he asked, his glowing eyes fixed on the decorations.

"It's a tradition," Max's dad explained. "We decorate the tree to make it beautiful and special for Christmas."

Zorb nodded thoughtfully. "On my planet, we celebrate Luminafest by adorning our homes with glowing crystals. Perhaps this is similar."

"Sort of!" Max said. "Here, Christmas is about spreading joy, love, and kindness. It's the most wonderful time of the year."

After the tree was decorated, Max's mom brought out a tray of freshly baked cookies. The warm, sugary scent made Zorb's antennae twitch. "What are these?" he asked.

"Christmas cookies," Lily said, handing him one shaped like a snowflake. "Try one!"

Zorb hesitated but took a small bite. His eyes widened, and his skin briefly glowed brighter. "Delightful! This substance brings great satisfaction."

Max laughed. "That's the point. We make cookies to share with friends and neighbours. It's one way we spread Christmas cheer."

"Sharing," Zorb repeated, making a note in his translator. "An admirable concept."

The next stop on Zorb's Christmas tour was the ice-skating rink. Max's family loaned him a pair of skates, though they had to adjust them to fit Zorb's three-toed feet. Zorb wobbled unsteadily as he stepped onto the ice, his long limbs flailing.

"This surface is unstable!" he exclaimed, slipping and sliding as Max and Lily laughed.

"You'll get the hang of it," Max said, taking Zorb's hand. "Just move your feet like this."

With their help, Zorb managed to glide across the ice, though not without a few comical tumbles. By the time they left, his laughter echoed through the night. "This activity brings joy through shared challenges," Zorb said, nodding appreciatively. "I understand its purpose."

As the evening grew late, Max suggested one final stop: the town's annual Christmas market. The square was alive with stalls selling handmade ornaments, warm cider, and knitted scarves. A choir sang carols near a roaring fire, and the air buzzed with excitement.

"This is the heart of Christmas," Max said as they wandered through the market. "It's about coming together."

Zorb marvelled at the sights and sounds. He observed families laughing, friends exchanging gifts, and strangers wishing each other a Merry Christmas. "Your people find happiness in togetherness," he said. "This is a powerful tradition."

Max grinned. "Exactly. That's what Christmas is all about."

Before Zorb returned to his ship, Max's family gathered one last time to exchange gifts. Max handed Zorb a small wrapped package. "This is for you," he said.

Zorb opened it carefully, revealing a tiny snow globe with a miniature Christmas tree inside. He shook it, and the glittery snow swirled around. "A remarkable object," Zorb said. "What does it signify?"

"It's a memory," Max said. "Something to remind you of your first Christmas on Earth."

Zorb's glowing eyes softened. "I will treasure it."

As he prepared to leave, Zorb turned to Max and his family. "Your Christmas traditions have taught me much about your people. You value kindness, joy, and unity. These are qualities worth sharing across the galaxy."

Max beamed. "Maybe you can bring a little Christmas spirit back to your planet."

Zorb nodded. "I will. And perhaps I will return to learn more next year."

As Zorb's ship rose into the starry sky, Max and his family watched until it disappeared. They smiled, knowing they had given their unusual visitor a Christmas he would never forget.

And somewhere in the vast reaches of space, Zorb began planning how to introduce his fellow Luminarans to the magic of Christmas.

The End

Chapter 36: The Reverse Christmas

It was early Christmas morning at the North Pole, and Santa was just waking up from his busiest night of the year. After traveling the world in his sleigh, delivering gifts to children everywhere, he usually spent Christmas Day relaxing by the fire with Mrs. Claus, sipping hot cocoa, and sharing stories with the elves.

But this Christmas morning was different.

As Santa stretched and yawned, he noticed something unusual at the foot of his bed: a brightly wrapped present with his name on it. Santa blinked in surprise, rubbing his eyes. "Am I seeing things?" he muttered, leaning closer to inspect the gift.

On the tag, written in cheerful, colorful letters, was a simple message: For Santa, with love.

Santa chuckled, his belly shaking like a bowl full of jelly. "Well, this is unexpected. I wonder who could have left it here?"

Mrs. Claus walked in, carrying a tray of warm cinnamon rolls. When she saw the gift, she smiled. "What's that, dear?"

"It's for me!" Santa said, holding up the box. "I don't know where it came from."

Mrs. Claus tilted her head, then laughed softly. "Well, you've spent centuries giving to others. Maybe it's about time someone gave back to you."

As Santa unwrapped the gift, a chorus of giggles echoed from the hallway. Santa and Mrs. Claus turned to see a group of elves peeking around the corner, their faces alight with excitement.

"Was it you, my clever little helpers?" Santa asked, holding up the box.

The head elf, Jingle, stepped forward, shaking his head. "Not us, Santa. But we think you'll find out soon enough."

Curious, Santa opened the gift to reveal a beautiful handmade scrapbook. Inside were pages filled with drawings, letters, and photos from children around the world. Each page was a heartfelt message of thanks for the joy Santa had brought them.

One page had a crayon drawing of Santa flying his sleigh, with the words: Thank you, Santa! You make Christmas magical! – Emma, age 6.

Another had a letter that read: Dear Santa, you brought me my favorite toy last year. I hope you have a great Christmas, too! Love, Ravi.

Santa's eyes misted over as he flipped through the pages. "All these children... they thought of me?"

"They sure did," Jingle said, grinning. "This year, they decided to give you a Christmas to remember."

As Santa made his way downstairs, he was met with even more surprises. The great hall of the workshop was filled with presents, each wrapped and labelled with his name. The elves stood proudly by a towering Christmas tree, which sparkled with ornaments and twinkling lights.

"Happy Reverse Christmas, Santa!" the elves cheered.

"Reverse Christmas?" Santa repeated, his eyes twinkling with amusement.

"Yes!" Jingle said. "This year, the kids—and us elves—wanted to show you how much you mean to everyone. You've spent your whole life giving, so now it's your turn to receive."

Santa chuckled, shaking his head. "You've all outdone yourselves. I don't know what to say."

One by one, Santa opened the gifts. There was a scarf knitted by Mrs. Jones, the town baker, who had left it in her chimney with a note. A wooden carving of Santa's sleigh, made by a little boy named Noah. Even a box of cookies, carefully baked and decorated by a family in Norway, with a note that said: For Santa, because cookies aren't just for Christmas Eve.

Each gift was simple but heartfelt, and Santa's heart swelled with gratitude.

As he opened the last present—a beautiful red mug with the words Best Santa Ever painted on it—Santa stood and looked around at the elves, Mrs. Claus, and the glittering tree.

"You've all given me the best Christmas I could ever ask for," he said, his voice warm. "It's not about the gifts—it's about the love and thought behind them. I spend every year bringing joy to others, but this year, you've reminded me just how much joy there is in being loved."

For the rest of the day, Santa and the elves celebrated in true Christmas fashion. They played games, shared stories, and sang carols around the glowing tree. Santa even used his new mug to enjoy an extra-large cup of cocoa.

And as the stars twinkled in the crisp North Pole sky that night, Santa sat by the fire with Mrs. Claus, flipping through the scrapbook one more time. His heart was full, his spirit renewed, and he couldn't stop smiling.

"This Reverse Christmas," Santa said softly, "was the best surprise of all."

The End

Chapter 37: The Children and the Spirit of Christmas

In a quiet little town nestled between rolling hills, Christmas had always been a time of joy. Houses sparkled with lights, carolers sang through the streets, and the scent of gingerbread filled every home. But this year, something felt different. The usual buzz of excitement was missing, and the town square, once the heart of holiday cheer, stood dark and silent.

At the edge of town, a group of children gathered around the old oak tree where they always met after school. Clara, the oldest and the leader of their group, looked at her friends with a determined expression. "Christmas doesn't feel the same this year," she said. "Everyone seems so busy or worried. It's like the spirit of Christmas is gone."

"We have to do something!" said Ben, his eyes wide with urgency. "Christmas is supposed to be about happiness and magic."

"But what can we do?" asked Emma, her voice small. "We're just kids."

Clara smiled. "We might be just kids, but that doesn't mean we can't remind the town what Christmas is really about."

The next day, the children set to work. Clara had an idea to bring the spirit of Christmas back by doing small acts of kindness around the town. They started by gathering items from their homes—old scarves, mittens, and toys they no longer needed. With help from their parents, they baked cookies and made simple decorations from paper and pinecones.

Their first stop was Mrs. Green's house. She was the oldest person in town and rarely left her home anymore. Clara knocked on her door, holding a basket of cookies wrapped in a red ribbon. When Mrs. Green opened the door, her face lit up. "For me?" she asked, her voice trembling.

"Yes," Clara said with a smile. "Merry Christmas, Mrs. Green."

Tears welled in Mrs. Green's eyes as she took the basket. "Thank you, children. You've made my day."

Next, the children went to the town square. Together, they hung paper snowflakes from the lampposts and placed small pinecone decorations on every bench. Ben brought an old sled from his attic and turned it into a donation box for toys and clothes. A sign above it read: For those in need this Christmas.

Passersby stopped to watch, their curiosity growing. "What are you kids up to?" asked Mr. Taylor, the town carpenter.

"Bringing back the spirit of Christmas," Emma said proudly.

Mr. Taylor chuckled, but as he looked around at their work, his expression softened. "Well, I might have some extra lights at home. Let me go get them."

Soon, other townsfolk began pitching in. Mrs. Carter brought strings of lights to drape around the square, and the baker donated trays of warm bread to share with those who needed it. Even the mayor stopped by, promising to bring hot cocoa for everyone that evening.

By sunset, the square was transformed. The children's simple decorations, combined with the townsfolk's contributions, had created something magical. The square glowed with soft lights, and the donation box was overflowing with gifts. A tall pine tree stood in the center, its branches adorned with handmade ornaments and shining stars.

As the townsfolk gathered, Clara stood on a small crate to address them. "Christmas isn't about fancy gifts or perfect decorations," she said, her voice clear and steady. "It's about kindness, love, and helping each other. We wanted to remind everyone of that."

The crowd erupted into cheers, and the children beamed with pride. Someone began to sing a carol, and soon everyone joined in, their voices rising into the crisp winter air.

As the stars appeared in the night sky, Clara looked around at the glowing square and the smiling faces of her neighbors. "We did it," she whispered to her friends.

"You mean we all did it," Ben said, gesturing to the crowd.

That night, the spirit of Christmas returned to the little town, not through grand gestures or expensive gifts, but through the small, heartfelt actions of children who believed in its magic.

And from that year on, the town never forgot the lesson the children had taught them: the spirit of Christmas lives in every act of kindness, no matter how small.

The End

Disclaimer

The stories in The Snowflake Chronicles: 37 Christmas Adventures are works of fiction, created to inspire joy, imagination, and holiday spirit. Any resemblance to actual events, people, or places is purely coincidental. These tales are intended for entertainment and family enjoyment and are suitable for children of all ages.

While great care has been taken to ensure the content is appropriate and heartwarming, the author and publisher recommend that parents or guardians preview the stories to ensure they align with their family's preferences and values.

This book may not be reproduced, stored in a retrieval system, or transmitted in any form or by any means—electronic, mechanical, photocopying, recording, or otherwise—without prior written permission from the author or publisher.

Enjoy the magic of the season responsibly, and may the spirit of Christmas bring happiness and togetherness to your family.

Warm holiday wishes,

Milton Keynes UK
Ingram Content Group UK Ltd.
UKHW031045291124
451807UK00001B/101

9 798230 425243